D0546506

That's
Mr. Faggot
to You

ALSO FROM ALYSON
BY MICHAEL THOMAS FORD

Alec Baldwin Doesn't
Love Me
and Other Trials
From My Queer Life

That's
Mr. Faggot
to You

FURTHER TRIALS FROM
MY QUEER LIFE

MICHAEL THOMAS FORD

alyson books
los angeles | new york

© 1999 BY MICHAEL THOMAS FORD. ALL RIGHTS RESERVED.

MANUFACTURED IN THE UNITED STATES OF AMERICA.

THIS TRADE PAPERBACK ORIGINAL IS PUBLISHED BY ALYSON PUBLICATIONS,
P.O. BOX 4371, LOS ANGELES, CALIFORNIA 90078-4371.
DISTRIBUTION IN THE UNITED KINGDOM
BY TURNAROUND PUBLISHER SERVICES LTD.,
UNIT 3 OLYMPIA TRADING ESTATE, COBURG ROAD, WOOD GREEN,
LONDON N22 6TZ ENGLAND.

FIRST EDITION: JUNE 1999

99 00 01 02 03 **a** 10 9 8 7 6 5 4 3 2

ISBN 1-55583-496-5

LIBRARY OF CONGRESS CATALOGING-IN-PUBLICATION DATA
FORD, MICHAEL THOMAS.
    THAT'S MR. FAGGOT TO YOU : FURTHER TRIALS FROM MY QUEER LIFE /
MICHAEL THOMAS FORD.—1ST ED.
    ISBN 1-55583-496-5
    1. HOMOSEXUALITY—HUMOR. 2. GAY MEN—HUMOR. 3. GAY WIT AND
HUMOR. I. TITLE. II. TITLE: THAT'S MISTER FAGGOT TO YOU.
PN6231.H57F68 1999
814'.54—DC21   98-54290 CIP

COVER PHOTOGRAPH BY PETER URBAN.

For Robrt Pela,
a man of few vowels and much good advice

Contents

Part Four: God Is Dog Spelled Backward

Part Five: Our Queer Lives

Author's Note

In general, writers write in solitude. We put our words onto paper and send them out into the world without really knowing what happens to them. But sometimes we are lucky enough to find out. After publication of my last essay collection, *Alec Baldwin Doesn't Love Me and Other Trials From My Queer Life,* I had the pleasure of traveling all around the country doing readings and meeting the men and women who had bought my book. I also received hundreds of letters and E-mails from people who had read the book and enjoyed it. And one from some guy who didn't enjoy it and wanted his money back, but we won't talk about that.

This second collection of essays is possible because so many of you enjoyed the first, and for that I am very thankful. I am also indebted to the owners and managers of the lesbian and gay bookstores who invited me to read, and to the many queer newspapers, radio shows, and television programs that were kind enough to review the book or interview me. Your support was invaluable in making the last book a success.

Personal thanks must also go to the many people who helped me out in various ways during the last year by providing friendship, dispensing words of wisdom, or giving me a place to stay on my wanderings. Among my personal saints are Linda Smukler and Susan Fox Rogers, Alex

Samuelson, Emma Dryden and Anne Corvi, Thomas Roche, Diane Fraser and Rudy, Gerry Kroll, Mark David Fennell, Michael Rowe and Brian McDermid, Paul J. Williams, Peter McKie, Nancy Garden, Katherine Gleason, and the incomparable Doug Rose.

Finally, my ongoing thanks to the newspaper and magazine editors who continue to run my columns every month, to Alec Baldwin for being such a good sport, and to the folks at Alyson for doing this all again. And a special thanks to my dog, Roger. I'm sorry I had to leave you so many times. It's OK about the rug.

Oh, and by the way, that *is* me on the cover of the book. I know I swore I would never do it, but all the porn stars were busy that day and we had to have *something*.

Part One

Just Another Day

Straight Talk

It's Friday night, and I am standing in the local video store, staring at the wall of rentals. My eyes are glazed over from having looked at the same 20 boxes for 15 minutes, and I'm in a bit of a panic because more alert browsers are quickly snatching up anything worth watching. I'm trying to decide between something that looks interesting but is potentially really awful (otherwise known as Critically Praised Foreign Film with Attractive Cover Art But No Discernible Plot) or something that features Bruce Willis's chest and is therefore a sure thing.

As I waffle between the two, a pair of girls scampers down the aisle, giggling wildly. About eight or nine, they are both wearing Pete's Pizza Parlor junior league soccer jerseys sporting fresh grass stains. Apparently having just won their early evening game, they are clutching wrinkled dollar bills in their hands and have clearly been put in charge of choosing the film for the evening's celebration.

The first girl, a tomboy type whose aggressive demeanor and missing front teeth suggest that she is probably the captain of the Pete's Pizza team, goes immediately for the latest Disney movie featuring talking animals, tap-dancing flatware, and songs that will make her parents' ears ring permanently after hearing them sung 15 billion times over the next two days. But the second, a pigtailed redhead with strawberry spots all over her happy face, is more careful. She scans each of the rows for the perfect selection, thoughtfully reading the descriptions on the back of each box.

Finally she picks one. "I want to see this," she says, presenting her friend with her choice. She's holding *The Incredibly True Adventure of Two Girls in Love.* Intrigued by her selection, I wait to see what happens next.

"Eww," says her friend after glancing at the cover. "I don't want to see that. It's about lezzies. Lezzies are disgusting. You aren't a lesbo, are you?" Her face is wrinkled in disgust, and she shoves the box back into her friend's hand as if it were something covered in filth, staring at her with a look that implies that answering her question in the affirmative will bring dire consequences.

The pigtailed girl blushes but doesn't say anything. She quickly puts her movie back and picks up the Disney. Her friend grins, seemingly satisfied, but the empty spaces in her mouth form darkened windows in her smile. The redheaded girl glances at the movie in her hands and says, "I guess this is OK." As they walk to the counter to pay, she looks back wistfully at her first choice, still sitting on the shelf.

This scene stays with me throughout the week, popping into my head during quiet moments. And each time it does, I get angry as I think about the way the red-haired girl was forced to give in to her friend. Certainly at eight or nine the little girl with the missing teeth cannot be accused of out-and-out conscious homophobia, but I find myself blaming her somehow for her innate sense of heterosexuality as preferred status.

Perhaps because of this, I start to become more and more aware of the intrusion of straight society into my world. I start keeping lists and quickly come up with the following examples:

I am riding the bus home one night. In front of me are two teenage boys. A few seats ahead of them are a couple of obviously gay men, having an animated conversation.

"I hate queers," says one of the boys out of the blue. "They make me sick."

"Yeah," says his friend angrily. "I'd like to kill all of them."

The gay men, oblivious to the hatred seething just a few rows behind them, stand up and ring for the next stop. The two boys watch them get off.

"Faggots," says the first one, watching the men through the window. "I bet they're going to that faggot restaurant over there."

The restaurant in question is a macrobiotic place that, while certainly familiar to my town's gay population, is hardly a queer hangout. In fact, its core clientele is largely heterosexual couples with digestive problems and pale girls who write bad poetry in battered notebooks.

"Yeah," says his friend as the bus pulls away. "All them homos eat that health food shit."

I watch the backs of their heads as the bus pulls up to my stop, wondering what they would do if I smacked them really hard. As I stand to get off the bus, I lean down and say, "You know, some of us homos eat the same crap you two do," and watch their jaws drop.

I go to visit my sister, who has recently taken a job in the pet store of her small country town, where she sells birds. Her coworker and new best friend is a woman named Mandy, who is five feet tall and weighs more than 300 pounds. We talk for a while about the birds, which chatter ceaselessly and which both my sister and Mandy adore. I find them annoying and excuse myself. After I leave, Mandy tells my sister that she thinks I'm cute.

"Forget it," my sister tells her. "He won't go out with you."

"Because I'm fat?" says Mandy, who is apparently used to being given that reason.

"Because he likes guys," my sister says.

Mandy sighs. "What a waste," she says. "Why are all the good ones gay?"

I know the details of this conversation because my sister tells them to me. Repeatedly. For the next month, every time she calls she has to remind me that Mandy thinks it's such a waste that I'm gay.

"Isn't that the funniest thing you've ever heard?" she says each time.

It's another morning at the park, where I take my dog for his daily swim. One of the regulars, Dave, is talking to another, Bill, about an upcoming business trip Bill is making to San Francisco.

"Man, you have to go this place," Dave tells Bill. "It's called Castro. Weird as all hell, but you can get really great haircuts there. Just watch out for all the freaks walking around."

Bill takes out a piece of paper and writes this down. "Castro," he repeats as he writes. "As in Fidel Castro?"

"I don't know," Dave answers. "There are a lot of guys in leather there. I don't know why. But you should go. It's really freaky."

"They're wearing leather because they're gay," I say, and both Dave and Bill stare at me blankly.

"*The* Castro," I tell them. "It's the gayest part of San Francisco."

"Oh," says Dave finally. "I guess that explains why it's so weird. Anyway, you can get great haircuts there."

I am talking to one of my editors on the phone. She is working on the manuscript of my new book for young adults, a collection of interviews with lesbian and gay people.

"It's great," she says, but underneath her words is that familiar tone that means something else is coming.

"But?" I say, prompting her.

"Well, we'd like to take out the interview with the transvestite."

"He's a transsexual," I say. "Not a transvestite."

"Oh," she says. "Is there a difference? Anyway, we think it's far too controversial. And it's not like there are a lot of them out there. The book will get more attention if we stick to plain old gay people."

I weigh the advantages and disadvantages of arguing with her about exactly what plain old gay people are. I think about my transsexual friends and how they looked for images of themselves as young people, finding nothing. The entire point of this book is to give young people examples of what might be possible in their lives. I start to say something.

"The publisher is very insistent on not asking for trouble," she says before I can reason with her. "Remember, your last book was banned in three cities." This is true. I found out about it when it was announced on CNN one evening and my mother called to tell me.

"Fine," I say, having heard this tone from her before and knowing that the decision has already been made. "Whatever."

Later that same day, my agent calls. There's bad news about a book proposal that she's been shopping around, a collection of essays by well-known gay writers talking about issues of aging in the queer community.

"Everyone thinks it's a depressing topic," she says. "They want gay romances. You know, like Gordon Merrick. Can you write something like that?"

Gordon Merrick. His were the first books I ever read about gay people, when I was 12. I bought them at the local Waldenbooks while my father waited behind me, oblivious, and the salespeople showed one another my purchases and snickered. At home I locked myself in my bedroom and devoured them. I was thrilled by the descriptions of sex, but wondered if I really had to take so many drugs and be as unhappy as the men in Merrick's world.

"No," I tell my agent. "I don't really think I can write something like that."

I keep recording these examples throughout the summer, and the quickness with which they accumulate is both disconcerting and annoying. I start to realize that to most people, I am invisible as a gay man. There are no identifying signs that mark me as being anything other than one of the thousands of other Irish men who walk down Boston's streets in shorts and baseball caps. Even the tattoo of interlocking Mars symbols on my right shoulder is invisible unless I'm changing at the gym.

On the one hand, this anonymity means that I live relatively free of the problems faced by some queer people who are more visibly out. Apart from the neighbor boys who once stole my rainbow flag from my porch, I do not get harassed because of who I am. I haven't been called a faggot since high school, and thankfully I have never felt threatened walking down the street.

But being invisible also has its disadvantages, and by the time fall rolls around, I've had enough. None of the encounters I've had with straight people have been enough in and of themselves to defeat me, but their accumulated weight has made me, well, just a little bit edgy about heterosexuals. I'm tired of being around them. I need to be with my own kind for a while.

I decide to go on a weekend camping retreat with a pagan group I belong to. While the group is not precisely gay, there are a lot of us in attendance, and even the ones who aren't might as well be, given the atmosphere of tolerance that pervades such events. It's relaxing. My guard is down. I don't feel like smacking anyone for four whole days. At least not out of anger.

There is a man at the gathering whom I find very attractive, but I just don't have the energy to pursue him. My recent brushes with heterosexuality have made me wary of sex in general. I decide I will use the weekend to regroup and recover, to ready myself for a return to the real world. Besides, I manage to find out, he lives halfway across the country. While a weekend of great sex would be welcome, I dismiss it as impractical.

On Monday afternoon, while packing the car to leave, I discover that this man and I have a mutual friend. We end up talking.

"It's too bad we didn't meet earlier," he says. "I noticed you the first night, but I didn't want to say anything."

"Why not?" I ask. Even though I thought the same thing about him, I am, of course, anxious that something about me prevented him from being as forward as he would have liked.

"Well," he says. "I thought you were straight."

As Mandy would say, what a waste.

Guy Problems

A couple of Wednesdays ago, my sister called for our semiweekly chat. We spoke for a while, and after we'd caught up on the latest news and she had filled me in on the details of her breakup with the most recent unsuitable boyfriend, she asked me to hang on for a second. I heard voices in the background, and when Karen returned, she said, "Jack has something he wants to talk to you about."

Jack is her son and, due to the laws of relativity, my nephew. Some readers may remember him from previous columns as the young man who has shown an inordinate amount of interest in show tunes. Well, he's now 12 and entering middle school. While I find this difficult to believe, probably wanting to maintain the illusion that he is still five and I am not hurtling rapidly toward 30, the fact is, Jack is starting to encounter all of those pleasant adolescent hurdles like acne, voice changes, and, as I was soon to find out, more difficult challenges.

"You have to leave," Jack said to my sister after picking up the phone. "This is guy stuff."

Karen dutifully exited the room, and as soon as she was gone, Jack breathed heavily into the receiver. "I have a problem," he said. "A big problem."

"I told you last time, everybody does it," I said reassuringly. "Just make sure you lock the bathroom door this time. I don't think your mother has quite gotten over it yet."

"It isn't *that,*" Jack said impatiently. "It's even more important."

I couldn't imagine anything more important than *that,* at least not when I was 12. In fact, I don't know many guys under 60 who think there's anything more important than *that.* But maybe that's just me. At any rate, I was curious to hear what was going on in Jack's life that was so significant that it eclipsed even the forbidden joys of masturbation. So I sat patiently as his tale unraveled. It took him a good ten minutes to get it all out, but he managed. The result was worse than I'd imagined.

It seems he's involved in his first love triangle. Actually it's more of a love square, involving as it does three other 12-year-olds. As I was soon to discover, Jack has a crush on a young woman named Amber Platt, who he assures me is the most bewitching girl in his class. But he also thinks Megan Huckabone is rather swell, even if she is missing a front tooth from a confrontation with a softball. And standing in the middle of it all is Jack's best friend, Henry Bick, who also seems to think Megan is a cutie pie.

"So what do you think?" he asked me after he'd outlined in agonizing detail who liked whom and how much.

I stared at the diagram I'd made of the situation while he was talking. I am a visual person and like to have things in lists before I begin to think about them. Now I had all the participants lined up before me, but I was at a loss for words. To tell the truth, I'd been dreading this moment for a number of years. Jack's father is out of the picture, and I'm the one he comes to with dad-type problems. Most of them, like how to put on a jock for Little League or what to get his mom for Christmas, are easy enough to handle.

Even the masturbation discussion had been relatively easy. For some reason, I never think of jacking off as sex. It's more like playing a vigorous round of rock-paper-scissors or something. There's a certain amount of societal baggage attached to it, but ultimately it's just you and your hand and maybe some tissues. When Jack had brought up the subject of his own self-exploration, I'd been able to explain it to him calmly and reasonably, and I hadn't even blushed when I informed him that of course his mother did it too and that it wasn't anything to be ashamed about. Why, I told him, even the president does it. It was nothing to worry about.

This, however, was different. This went beyond sex for one and straight into uncharted territory. This was all about the first stirrings of pubescent desire and, well, I wasn't sure how to talk to him about, you know…girls. More specifically, I didn't know how to talk to him about what boys did with girls. Girls and girls I could do. Boys and boys as well. But this was the stuff that had made me queasy even as a kid, and now he was expecting me to help him figure it out. I couldn't tell him that I haven't even figured it out yet.

When Jack's father first left, Jack was very young, and I'd hoped that some other man would come along to take his place before he was old enough to wonder about things like this and ask me about them. I had also, given Jack's show tune fetish, thought that perhaps he might one day come to me with other, slightly different questions—ones I could answer with more authority. But despite numerous attempts, my sister had managed to remain single, and regardless of the show tune thing, Jack seemed to be developing at least some kind of curiosity about girls. So there I was, faced with his first big romantic question and no idea how to handle it.

"Well?" said Jack, bringing me back to the present. "Who should I go out with?"

"Um, I don't know," I said vaguely.

"But I have to pick one of them," Jack said plaintively. "I'm almost 13. I have to have a girlfriend soon. Everyone else already does."

"Wait until you're almost 30 and still don't have one," I said bitterly.

"How would you choose?" Jack asked.

"I'd pick the butchest one," I said automatically, thinking about my own personal proclivities in men.

"What?" said Jack.

"Never mind," I said.

It was rapidly dawning on me that Jack hadn't reached the sex part of the equation yet and was still trying to sort out the basic lineup. I was relieved that we wouldn't be delving into moister topics, at least not immediately, but I was still unsure of how to proceed. My own feeble adolescent attempt at heterosexuality had consisted entirely of slipping Bobbi Jo Wagner a note in English asking if she "wanted to go with me." Her response, "I like to go shopping with you, but that's it," was the first hard evidence that perhaps my romantic leanings lay elsewhere. If Jack is in fact a budding homo, I wanted to spare him the same experience. But in my heart I knew he had to go it alone.

"Look," I said finally. "Which one do you like the best?"

"Well, Amber is a great dancer," said Jack. "But Megan is really good at basketball, and you know that's my favorite sport."

Wondering if maybe Megan and Jack had more in common than either of them knew, I said, "Then go out with her." If nothing else, they could shoot free throws together.

"But what about Henry?" said Jack.

"You want to go out with Henry?" I asked happily, hoping that the conversation would take a more positive direction after all.

Jack sighed. "*I'm* not gay," he said. "What I mean is that Henry likes Megan, too."

We were back to square one. Wanting to be helpful, I tried to think about what I would do in the same situation. The problem was, the dating rules for gay men are slightly different than they are for grade-school children. Or, I thought, maybe they aren't so different after all. Maybe all I had to do was reverse the situation and half of the genders.

"Hold on a minute," I said to Jack. "I have to think this one through."

I then invented in my mind a theoretical situation involving my friend Ed and two guys at our gym, Jesse and Roberto. In my scenario, I liked Jesse, who had nice pecs and lingered near me in the showers once. Roberto was less well-defined but was always very friendly and told bad jokes that cracked me up so that I almost dropped the weights. Usually, and for completely shallow reasons, I would be more tempted by Jesse. But I knew that Ed also liked him. In fact, Ed thought Jesse was his dream man and talked about him at every opportunity. Decisions, decisions.

"Can't you just date them both?" I asked Jack in frustration. "Or maybe share? You know, switch on and off."

"No," he said firmly.

I went back to work, weighing my friendship with Ed against how my tongue would feel running along Jesse's beautiful chest. It would be wonderful. But then I pictured running into Ed in Provincetown and having all of his friends point at me. The word "slut" would be uttered. The weekend would be ruined for everyone. My mind raced as I went from envisioning nights in Jesse's arms to seeing Ed's dejected face as he spent yet another lonely evening watching *What Ever Happened to Baby Jane?* and downing pint after pint of Ben & Jerry's Heath Bar Crunch, gaining 50 pounds while Jesse and I made love to the serenading of Ella Fitzgerald.

It was an agonizing three minutes. But finally I gave in and went for Roberto, leaving Jesse to the man who really loved him. It was the hardest thing I ever had to do. But to my surprise, I felt great about my decision. And ultimately (at least in my version) it worked out fine after all. Ed was happy, and we were still friends. Best of all, I discovered that Roberto was not only funny but hung like a horse.

"Let Henry go with Jesse, I mean Megan," I told Jack quickly.

"Thanks," he said. "But how did you decide that?"

"Years of experience," I answered.

I hung up, very pleased that despite my lack of enthusiasm for heterosexuality, I had been able to use my own experiences to help out my nephew. Why, guy problems were guy problems, regardless of who the person creating the dilemma was or how many holes she or he had.

A few minutes later the phone rang again, interrupting a particularly enjoyable fantasy involving Roberto, some sweaty boxer shorts, and a locker room. Thinking it might be Jack needing more advice, I picked up. But it was my friend James.

"Hi," he said. "I need to talk to you about something. See, there are these two guys who like me, and I'm not sure which one…"

"Go with Amber Platt," I said quickly and hung up.

Stand by Your Man

The only difference between gay men and white trash women is gay men wear better shoes.

I can say this with authority because I grew up intimately acquainted with white trash. All of my friends lived in trailers surrounded by shifting mounds of discarded tires, rusted-out car skeletons, and barking mongrel dogs named Skoal or Jack Daniels. Their fathers were largely truck drivers, mechanics, or geniuses at beating the welfare system. Few had all of their teeth, and the girls rarely escaped junior high without getting pregnant at least once. The only thing that kept me from attaining white trash status myself was adequate dental care and the fact that my father had a job that didn't involve wearing an orange safety vest or using torque wrenches.

While white trash men are largely undistinguished, white trash women are remarkable for one thing—their unfailing ability to fall in love with precisely the wrong men. A white trash man's romantic needs are satisfied by finding a woman who knows how to remove underarm stains from white T-shirts and who considers Miracle Whip a major food group. The white trash woman, however, is slightly more romantic. Knowing full well that the hero of all the Harlequin romances she reads will never appear on her doorstep, she decides to find the next best thing. In general, that means a man with a multitude of personality defects and antisocial behaviors. The idea is to find the biggest challenge and stick with it, thus proving Tammy Wynette—the reigning empress of white trash—correct in her advice to stand by one's man, whatever the cost.

Somewhere along the line, a white trash woman looked up from the box of week-old doughnuts she bought for half price at the Shop N Save, gazed with half-opened eyes at the guests on the *Donahue* show she was watching, and realized that she could make a giant leap forward by finding and marrying a convicted murderer. Thus began an exciting new trend in the world of white trash women. With ranks of the incarcerated to choose from, a feeding frenzy began. Within months death row inmates across the land were receiving boxes of Rice Krispie treats and letters promising undying affection. After a brief spate of correspondence, love inevitably blossomed. Then began the round of talk shows, on which proud and defiant white trash women wept waterfalls of blue eye shadow as they explained to fascinated audiences how their men had been wronged and how they would stand by them come hell or high water, electric chair or lethal injection.

Gay men know just how those women feel. OK, at least I do. Many years ago, shortly after I had moved to New York, I was looking for a man. After having no luck through the usual routes, I decided that I would put a personal ad in *The Village Voice*. I spent a long time composing it, as I wanted to attract the perfect guy, the man of my dreams who would make me the happiest boy on Earth.

The ad I placed went as follows:

GWM, 22, seeks regular guy. Is there anyone out there who loves dogs and action movies and doesn't hang out in bars or like Streisand? If so, call me soon; I can't wait much longer. Rugby players and Bruce Willis a plus.

I thought my ad very clever. So, apparently, did a lot of men in New York. I received dozens of responses in my voice-mail box the day the ad appeared. That night I sat happily in my apartment, listening to man after man apply for the position of my next beau. I dutifully wrote down all of their statistics and phone numbers. Then I went through the list and circled potential candidates. By the end of the evening I had narrowed the field down to three finalists.

The next day I called all three of them and left messages on their machines. I decided the first one to call back would be the grand prize winner. When the phone rang, I picked it up, breathless with anticipation. It was my call from Mr. Right.

Mr. Right turned out to be a man called Chandler. He was, he told me, an avid outdoorsman. He enjoyed camping and hiking, and he just adored dogs. In fact, he had one of his very own, a retriever named Champ. He had a great voice and was very funny. He did confess that he owned the *Barbra Streisand Christmas Album,* but I forgave him when he informed me that he was also a writer. We talked for a while longer and set up a date for the next night.

I was nervous about meeting Chandler. After all, what if I wasn't at all attracted to him? What if he wasn't attracted to me? He seemed so perfect and, at 22, I was convinced that it was high time for me to fall wildly in love with someone. As I headed for the restaurant, I sensed that somehow my life was about to change in a very big way.

Chandler turned out to be extremely attractive. And he was attracted to me as well. I was so giddy with relief that I ignored the fact he was considerably older than I was, and also the fact that despite direct questioning, he never provided any details about exactly what kind of writing he did. I just looked at his beautiful smile and brushed these things aside.

The next morning I called my friend Peter to tell him about my great first date with my new husband. I described Chandler in minute detail, from his deep brown eyes to his hairy arms. Peter listened patiently, then broke in when I was rhapsodizing on the way Chandler drank his beer from the bottle and didn't use the glass.

"Wait a minute," he said. "What did you say Chandler's last name is?"

"Keene," I said. "Isn't it great? Just think, Michael Thomas Keene."

"Chandler Keene," Peter interrupted. "I knew something sounded familiar about that."

"Don't tell me you've slept with him," I said. I wanted to think that Chandler had saved himself just for me, and Peter and I had already had the unpleasant experience of discovering we'd once dated the same person.

"No," said Peter. "But there is something you should probably know about him."

"What's that?" I asked, wondering what Peter could possibly know about my perfect boyfriend.

"He's a felon," Peter responded simply.

"A what?" I said, thinking I couldn't possibly have heard correctly.

"A convicted felon," Peter said slowly. "I remember it from the papers."

"But he said he was a writer," I protested.

"Oh, he was," said Peter gleefully. "He wrote a stock column for a financial paper. Only he was being paid off by different corporations to push their stocks. He made quite a bit of money at it. Until they caught him, anyway."

"And what happened to him?" I asked.

"He went to jail for about three or four years," Peter said. "He also wrote a book about the whole thing. I have a copy if you want to read it."

Of course I wanted to read it. After work I went over

and borrowed it from Peter, then spent the rest of the night finding out the truth about my man. As I turned the pages, his sordid story unfolded in graphic detail. I learned all about the bribes, the secret meetings, the illegal activities, the arrest and conviction. It was all there in black and white—I was dating one of the most notorious white-collar criminals the financial world had ever seen.

When I was done with the book, I turned it over and looked at the author photo on the back. There was Chandler's smiling face, just as I remembered it from the night before. I looked into those beautiful eyes, which seemed to be looking straight into my soul, and I forgave him. I forgave him everything. After all, he'd only stolen money from rich people. It wasn't like he'd actually killed anyone or bashed an old woman over the head or something. It was just shuffling pieces of paper around. Yes, it was a federal offense, but so were lots of other things that didn't seem like such big deals.

Besides, I was already picturing him in his prison uniform. I saw myself sitting with the other prison widows outside the rows of greasy telephones at the New York Correctional Facility. While we waited for our turns at the phones, we would compare stories.

"What's yours in for?" I would ask the lady next to me, a big-haired New Jersey trailer park housewife with too-tight jeans and a baggy sweater.

"Grand theft auto," she would answer. "But it was all a setup."

"I know how you feel," I'd say as I took her hand and patted it gently. "It's hard when they're on the inside and we're out here. No one understands the pain except someone who's been there."

"Ain't that the truth," my new friend would say. Then she would open her purse and take out the pictures of the children. There would be Billy, age 13 and turning into the man of the house. Then 11-year-old Eileen, who was a handful what with her no-good boyfriend and all. But saddest of all would be little Frank Jr., who was having his sixth birthday that very afternoon without his daddy.

Sniffling, I would show her a snapshot of Chandler and me and Champ on our last camping trip before Chandler had to go into the big house. "Champ and I still go to the woods sometimes," I would say. "But no one throws a ball for him like his daddy."

My daydream was very vivid, and even though Chandler's time in the pen was long over, I knew I would stick by him should it ever happen again. Secretly, I think I hoped it *would* happen again, just so I could experience the sheer heartache of pining for my incarcerated man. By the time I finally went to sleep that night, I was already making him homemade fudge to give to his cellmates.

When Chandler and I had our next date, I told him that I'd read his book.

"Oh, that," he said, as if it were nothing. "I'm glad that's all behind me now."

"It must have been terrible," I said sympathetically, so that he would know I had explored the depths of his pain and come back more committed to him than ever.

"Not really," he said. "Basically, I worked in the prison library and used the time to write my book. I lived better there than I ever did outside. Now I actually have to work for a living. *That's* what really sucks."

This was not what I wanted to hear. I wanted stories about knife fights and surly guards who demanded kickbacks for protection. I wanted to hear about staking out territory in the yard and narrowly escaping being some thug's bitch. But all Chandler had to say about his stay in the clink was that the cook used too much pepper in the gumbo. It was a bitter disappointment, and after a few more dates I broke things off.

I should have learned my lesson from that little escapade, but sometimes I still find myself longing for the touch of a bad boy. Several months ago, while watching one of those true-crime shows on television, I saw a profile of a man wanted in connection with the murder of several people in Alabama or somewhere. Of course I was appalled at what he'd done. Then they showed his picture. Despite my horror at his brutal behavior, I couldn't help but think he was really hot. Maybe, I reasoned, it had all been a big mistake. He looked like such a nice man. It was a passing thought, and I soon forgot about it.

A few days later, however, I turned on the evening news, only to hear a special bulletin that an escaped convict had been found right here in Boston. Then a picture of the very same man I'd seen on the crime show flashed on the screen. He was being led away in handcuffs, his handsome face looking down at his feet. I found myself wondering what would have happened if I'd met him somewhere before his arrest. Would I, like those big-haired, raccoon-eyed women telling their stories to Geraldo, have fallen for his seductive smile and lying eyes? Would I have pledged my love to him through a bullet-proof window and sent him packages of chocolate chip cookies and Polaroids of my naked self? Would I, indeed, have stood by my man? For a moment it all seemed terribly romantic. I think we're all lucky I never got the chance to find out.

At least I know I'm not the only gay man with white trash tendencies. When the whole Andrew Cunanan thing was happening, I received a call from my friend David.

"Can you believe this?" he said, shocked.

"It's terrible," I said sympathetically.

There was a pause.

"He is sort of cute, though, isn't he?" said David.

I knew where this was heading.

"He's not my type," I said cautiously.

"I don't know," said David. "I kind of like his preppy look in that mug shot. And with his head shaved, he looks so butch, don't you think?"

"David," I said reasonably. "The man killed four people, including Versace."

David sighed. I imagined him wiping his eyes as Sally Jessy handed him a tissue and the cameraman zoomed in for a close-up. "I know," he said plaintively. "But I'm sure he had a good reason. He probably just needs someone to care. And anyway, it wasn't like it was Armani."

Now I know why the Florida police were slow to put up posters of Cunanan when they knew he was in South Beach. They weren't afraid of causing a panic; they were afraid someone would start a fan club.

The Perils of P.E.

Summer is here, and I should be in shape. I even promised myself that this year I'd go to the gym and just do it. But once again I'm not ready. My stomach is still too big, my shoulders too small. Blame it on Wally Shufelt.

Wally Shufelt—Mr. Shufelt—was my fifth grade gym teacher. One of those aging ex-jocks who failed to make it to the majors, he told us at least once a month how the Dodgers almost signed him right out of high school but a knee accident sidelined him before the start of spring training. Instead, he spent his years taking out his frustrations on the boys he used to be, dedicating his life to making men of us. And he took to it with a fervor generally found only in missionaries and defenders of the spotted owl.

I think for most gay men gym class was a black or white thing. For those of us who could actually do things like tackle, hit balls, and sink free throws, it was a junior version of nirvana, complete with sweaty bodies and blossoming hormones. For those of us completely bereft of any coordination whatsoever, it was a different story altogether.

Today I can enjoy physical activity—I have even been known to watch sporting events from time to time—but back in my school days I was decidedly in the second camp. Although my father had been the star athlete at the same school 25 years earlier, I inherited none of his talent. And in a backwoods school where excelling in academics was nothing compared to being able to score 42 points in the first half of whatever game one was playing, this was a decided disadvantage.

How I dreaded those alternating days when fourth period came and I had to enter that cavernous, wooden-floored palace of misery with its stench of varnish and unwashed adolescence. Many were the mornings when I would wait for the bus and pray as hard as I could for God to bring about the Second Coming before 11:00 rolled around and I was forced to see what new ordeal Mr. Shufelt had prepared especially for me.

You see, although we engaged in the usual seasonal gym class cycle of soccer–basketball–baseball, Mr. Shufelt was happiest when putting us through the paces of some activity of his own design. He was of the firm opinion that athletics must involve 1) the hurling of some kind of solid object at a target, 2) winners and losers, and 3) pain. His favorite activities featured all three of his sports criteria, and the crowning jewel in his jockstrap was bombardment.

This clever game involved first dividing the class into two teams. Placed at opposite sides of the gym, we would wait, twitching with terror or anticipation depending upon our natures, as Mr. Shufelt walked into the center of the gym holding seven hard rubber balls. When he dropped them and blew his whistle, we would run as quickly as possible to snatch them up.

Then the slaughter began.

The object of bombardment was, essentially, to kill one another by throwing the balls with terrific force at your opponents. If you were hit, you were out. If you caught the ball thrown at you, whoever threw it was out. Eventually only two people would be left to face off against each other like gladiators in a ring.

In theory this game could be amusing. In reality it was a bloodbath, especially for the small and uncoordinated. Since having your ball caught would disqualify you, the larger boys avoided this potential embarrassment by pitching them with such force as to knock any reasonably sized target unconscious.

The obvious solution to the problem was to get hit as quickly as possible. I usually managed to do this within minutes of the game's beginning, taking a whack to the arm or chest and then dashing for the safety of the bleachers. On occasion I even managed to feign being struck by emitting a loud groan and limping slightly.

But one fateful day, things didn't go my way. I tried my best, but some evil angel seemed to be delivering me from shot after shot, even when I threw myself directly in the way of oncoming balls. Before I knew it, I was the last person on my team left on the floor. And I was face to face with Andy Peerson. Andy was the biggest kid in class. Rumored to be 23, he'd been left back so many times, his name filled up every line of the "This book belongs to:" section of his English textbook.

I stood looking at Andy and at the ball gripped tightly in his massive hand. Somehow I also had a ball in my hands. I had no how it had come to be there or what to do with it. I'd never gotten to hold one before.

"Hit him!" someone yelled from the sidelines. I wasn't sure if he was yelling at me or Andy.

Andy narrowed his eyes. I saw his huge arm rise up in the air, the ball held aloft. He let out a growl.

I closed my eyes and waited to die. Then I had an idea. In the split second before Andy threw, I could throw my ball and hit him in the legs. It wasn't the bravest way to end the standoff, but it would do, and I'd be a hero for once. On my deathbed, it would be the shining gym class moment I'd recall before passing on.

I opened my eyes and let fly my ball. I watched as it

sped toward Andy. My heart filled with joy.

Then he stepped aside. Just like that. My ball whizzed past him and smacked against the wall with a sad little plop.

Andy sneered and threw. I watched as the ball sailed toward me as if in slow motion. It hit me square in the head, and I fell down, my ears ringing and my eyes filled with stars. When I looked up. Mr. Shufelt was standing over me.

"Nice catch, Ford" he said mockingly. "Your team gets 50 push-ups for losing."

Nearly 20 years later, I still see Mr. Shufelt in my mind whenever I think about going to the gym. But confronted with the idea of spending yet another summer indoors because I haven't managed to get into swimsuit shape is enough to scare me out of my desk chair and into the nearest temple of body worship. I decide to overcome my fears once and for all.

I am fully aware that I am a lazy son of a bitch, and I know that I won't do so much as change into my shorts and sneakers without being forced to do so by someone else. I decide that my best course of action is to hire a personal trainer. It's hideously expensive, but I remind myself that since quitting therapy I have more disposable income. Besides, I like the idea of dropping the phrase "my personal trainer" into conversations, much as I used to think saying "my agent thinks I should try scripts" was a real kick.

I begin by looking through the local gay newspaper for a suitable candidate. There are two ads for personal trainers. One features a photo of a well-muscled man wearing a sleeveless flannel shirt and jeans unbuttoned at the crotch. The other ad has no photo. I stare at the first ad. I imagine staring at this man's crotch while he yells at me to "pump it." While this concept is not unappealing, I decide I need a trainer, not a porn star, and call the second ad.

My trainer's name is Paul. He does not wear flannel shirts or jeans open at the crotch, at least not when I meet him at the gym. He is very lively and encouraging, and although I find this disturbing at 7 in the morning, I try not to let it get to me. I'm having a hard enough time being in an actual gym wearing actual gym clothes. I find myself worrying that, like Mr. Shufelt, Paul will demand to know if I am wearing appropriate support gear. I decide to start off our conversation by informing him that I am.

Paul takes this in stride and tells me that we will begin our session by seeing just how fit or unfit I am. I chuckle at this, and tell him that I don't need any help knowing how unfit I am. But he perseveres, and minutes later I am standing in front of a rack of weights while Paul tells me the correct way to lift them.

"Aren't we going to just use those machines?" I ask, waving vaguely at the shiny rows of equipment that fill the gym.

"Those?" says Paul with disgust. "Those are for sissies. Real men use free weights."

Already I am feeling depressed. I have issues about weights, having been given a set for Christmas the year I was ten. I had been hoping for a giant stuffed lion, and was more than a little dismayed when I raced downstairs and found a barbell wrapped with a red bow sitting under the tree.

I feel the same way now as Paul has me lift the bar to get used to the heft of it. I manage to hoist it up to my waist and then to my chest as Paul keeps up a steady stream of encouragement. Then down it goes again, dropping into the receiving brackets with a clink.

"Good," says Paul. "Now we'll put some weight on it."

I watch, terrified, as he pulls two weights off the rack and slips them onto the ends of the bar. I was hoping we'd just stick with the empty steel rod for the first time. But Paul has other ideas. He puts two more weights on the bar, then tells me to lift it. I wrap my hands around the bar and pull up on it, tentatively testing the weight.

"Lift!" Paul bellows in my ear.

Caught off-guard, I propel the barbell up and over my head without even thinking. Then I stand there swaying slightly from side to side, not knowing what to do.

"Good man," says Paul, slapping me on the back. "Now you can put it back. But make sure you do it slowly. We don't want you to hurt yourself."

I think it's probably too late for that, but I lower the bar slowly until it's safely in its original position and I can let go.

I look at Paul, and he's writing something in a little notebook.

"This is your workout record," he says, noticing my quizzical look. "I'm writing down how much you can lift. This way we'll know how you progress."

"So what was that?" I ask. "A hundred? One twenty?"

Paul smiles. "A little less," he tells me, shutting the notebook with a slap. "Why don't we move on to some other things."

For the next hour Paul has me lifting and pulling on a variety of weights. I have no idea what any of them are doing, but I duly lift and press and put the weights back again, making sure never to drop them. By the time we end, I am feeling slightly better about this whole workout thing.

"Great," Paul tells me when we finish the last exercise. "Now let's try some cardio."

Trying some cardio, I come to find out, is Paul's way of saying he's going to make me run on a treadmill for 20 minutes. He wants to see if I can do it without fainting. At the five-minute mark, he asks how I'm doing.

"Am I supposed to taste blood in my throat?" I ask.

Paul turns off the treadmill, and we're finished for the day. He hands me the little notebook he has been scribbling in and pats me on the back again.

"Good work," he says cheerfully. "We'll have you in shape in no time."

I go home feeling proud of myself. I have survived an actual training session with an actual personal trainer. Surely I can't be all that hopeless. After all, I was able to lift the weights Paul asked me to without too much trouble. I feel very butch as I swing my gym bag and head for the subway. I imagine running into Mr. Shufelt on the street and kicking his ass, and I laugh.

Later that night, before going to bed, I empty my bag and discover the little notebook. Curious to see just how much I was lifting, I open it and take a peek at what Paul has written there. Almost instantly my good mood vanishes.

Next to the first exercise he's written in 60 pounds. Here I thought I'd been heaving a respectable 100 pounds over my head. But 60? That's the weight of a medium-sized Labrador. Why, my dog weighs 110, and I've picked him up before. But there it is in blue ballpoint. Sixty pathetic pounds. The rest of the numbers are equally depressing. I can't even look at them. I close the notebook and shove it into the bag where I won't have to look at it. Then I crawl into bed.

I fall asleep and immediately start to dream. I am walking toward the front door of the gym. As I open it and begin to step inside, I see all of the men turn from their treadmills and weight machines and pick up the rubber balls thrown into the middle of the gym. Stepping out of the shadows, Mr. Shufelt blows his whistle and I cover my head and scream as the sound of rushing air fills my ears.

When the alarm rings at 6 the next morning, every muscle in my body hurts. Crawling out of bed, I call Paul. I've decided that the gym thing just isn't for me. Luckily I get his answering machine. I leave a message saying that I have decided to enter a monastery after all and won't be needing his services. Then I stumble back to bed, pull the blankets over my head, and go back to sleep. This time I dream of nothing.

Where Have All the Flowers Gone?

It's official—romance is dead.

The tragic event occurred at 9:36 last Tuesday night. That was when a group of friends and I were sitting around in a bar after a reading in which several of us had taken part. Basking in the glow of postperformance relief, we were knocking back a few beers and talking about all of those important things that people talk about when they're slightly buzzed. We had already discussed which childhood comic book heroes we'd had crushes on, what our favorite songs of the 1970s were, and the relative appeal of corduroy pants. Now it was my turn to choose a topic for debate.

"Here you go," I said after thinking for a minute. "I want to talk about flowers."

"Flowers?" said my friend Anna. "What about them?"

Truth be told, I wanted their advice. I was thinking about sending flowers to a man I had recently met and was considering asking out, but I wasn't entirely sure it was the right thing to do. Not being the most adept dater, I find that it's always advisable to run my plans past people more experienced in romance than I am.

"Say you meet this guy," I theorized. "At a party or something. He seems really nice, and you have a great conversation. A couple of days later, you get flowers from him and a note saying he really enjoyed talking to you and would like to maybe have dinner or coffee or something."

"How did he get my address?" asked my friend Jackson suspiciously.

"What?" I said, momentarily caught off-guard. "I don't know. What difference does it make? That's not the point."

"I just wouldn't want any of you giving out my address or phone number to some guy who wanted to stalk me," he said.

"Who said anything about stalking?" I said. "It's just flowers. Besides, he's a friend of a friend, not just someone off the street."

"I don't know," said Anna, taking a drag on her cigarette. "It sounds like too much commitment to me. I mean, I feel like I owe a guy sex if he buys me dinner. Starting with flowers would be like asking me to swallow on the first date. I'm not ready for that."

"He just wants to have dinner!" I said. "No one even mentioned sex."

"It's always about sex," said Jackson bitterly. "A guy doesn't send flowers just to be nice. He wants sex. And if he wants sex, why can't he just call me and ask to come over? Why send flowers? What's that supposed to mean, anyway?"

"It doesn't have to *mean* anything," I explained in exasperation. "He likes you. He wants to tell you that, and he wants to ask you to dinner. What's the big deal about flowers? They're romantic."

"It's just sort of creepy," said Anna. "You know, desperate and clutchy and all that."

I couldn't believe what I was hearing. Granted, I am not exactly an expert in the area of interpersonal relationships, but I would be thrilled if someone sent me flowers. You know, as long as I liked him. But even if I didn't, I wouldn't turn him in to the local sex crimes unit. Apparently my friends felt differently.

"I don't like all that flowers and cards crap," said Jackson. "Next thing you know, he'll be calling my dad asking for my hand in marriage. I prefer your standard gay date—go to dinner and then go home and have sex all night. Say good-bye in the morning. Maybe exchange numbers if you want to do it again. That's it."

"Amen," said Anna.

"But you're a straight girl," I protested. "You're supposed to love all that romantic stuff."

"No one I know does," she insisted. "That's all just a cover-up for getting you into bed. Any girl I know would be really suspicious if some guy sent her flowers. He's trying too hard. It's like not waiting a day to call someone back."

"Waiting a day?" I asked, confused.

Anna sighed. "I forget that you're dating-challenged," she said. "It's the one day rule. You never call someone back the same day he calls you. That makes it look like you don't have anything better to do. But if you wait a day, then that makes him think you didn't get home early enough to return his call, like maybe you were having a fabulous night out at the opera or hanging out in SoHo with Robert De Niro or something. Then he thinks you're really fabulous and interesting."

"But what if he knows about the one day rule?" I said, cleverly thinking ahead.

"It doesn't matter," said Anna patiently. "Even if he does, he still won't know for sure if you didn't call him back because of that or because you really were out all night. So you win either way."

"OK, but what if you're both playing the one day rule. Then no one ever calls anyone."

"You're reading too much into this," said Jackson. "It's really not that difficult."

"*I'm* reading too much into this?" I said. "You're the one who thinks anyone who sends you flowers should be under psychiatric care."

"He should," said Jackson. "Or at least heavily medicated. I prefer my men to be the no-nonsense kind."

"I just don't get this," I said. "I can't be that behind the times."

"You are," said Anna. "I'll prove it to you. Let's take a little quiz. Question one. You've managed to ask someone out, and you're deciding what to do on your date. Where do you go?"

"To a movie and dinner," I answered confidently. That was an easy one.

"Wrong," said Anna instantly. "Jackson, tell him the right answer."

"Coffee," said Jackson. "Always coffee first. It's too much of a commitment to do anything more than that, and if things don't go well you can always leave after 20 minutes. With dinner you're talking at least an hour. Add a movie to it and there go three hours of your life."

"You do get two points for the movie idea, though," said Anna kindly. "At least if things are going badly you don't have to talk to the guy, and it might be something you wanted to see anyway. But don't even think about paying for his ticket unless you want him to run screaming for the nearest door."

"And no sharing popcorn, insisted Jackson. "You both buy your own."

"Gee, thanks," I said. "I'll try to remember not to scare anyone off by offering him a Milk Dud. OK. Next question."

"It's time for the first sexual get-together," Anna said. "Where do you go?"

I thought for a minute. I tried hard to remember everything I'd learned in my SAT preparation classes about picking the right answers by eliminating the obvi-

ously wrong ones. "Um, to my place?" I said finally, figuring I had a 50-50 chance of being right. I also thought
going to my place would be a nice gesture, a first step on
the road to intimacy.

"Wrong again," said Jackson. "You always go to his
place for the first time. That way you can check out what
it looks like and get clues about what kind of guy he is. I
like to go through their drawers while they're in the
shower. Once I found an entire scrapbook filled with
cutout pictures of Kate Jackson and poems about her
hair. We never had a second date."

"I always take a look in the refrigerator," added Anna.
"If it's got lots of leftovers, I know he's a loser who stays
home every night. But if there's nothing in there but
some moldy Brie and a bottle of flat seltzer, it's a go."

"So we go to his place so I can spy on him," I said,
making a mental note to throw out all of the Tupperware
containers in my fridge.

"Right," said Anna. "Besides, if you're at his place, you
can always leave afterwards. But if he's at your place, it's
harder to get him out."

"But what if I want him to stay?" I said.

Both Anna and Jackson shook their heads. "You
never stay over the first time," said Jackson. "You
shouldn't even think about staying over until at least the
seventh time."

"And even then, don't even think about bringing a
toothbrush with you," said Anna. "I know what you're
thinking. But that's just asking for trouble."

"Oh, here's a good one," said Jackson excitedly.
"Bonus question. You've been going out with this guy
once or twice a week for three months. One Friday night
you go out with some friends—say with us—and you see
him having dinner with someone else. What do you do?"

"If we've been going out for three months, shouldn't
we be spending Friday nights together?" I said, con-

fused. "Why is he out with someone else?"

"That's exactly what I thought you would say," crowed Jackson. "See, you're hopeless. You think a couple of months of dating means you're married."

"Well, it should mean *something*!" I said. "Why bother dating someone if it doesn't mean something after three months?"

"We can't put you into the dating pool," said Anna sadly. "You'll get eaten alive. Face it, you're doomed."

"Well, I don't believe you," I said. "There have to be some men left—and women too—who want romance. There have to be some people left who like being courted."

Anna and Jackson looked at each other and laughed cruelly.

"This is why you never go out with anyone," said Jackson. "You haven't learned the rules yet. Just screw 'em and get out. That's how it's done. If you happen to find one you want to keep around, don't blow it by sending him flowers or singing beneath his window or whatever stupid thing you have in mind. It'll just backfire. You have to play hard to get."

"You are a bitter queen," I said. "And I'm going to prove you wrong. Both of you."

The next day, I called up the local florist and sent the man I was interested in a dozen roses with a card that read, "I've enjoyed getting to know you. How about dinner on Friday?"

Then I waited. I knew he'd call. After all, since meeting we'd spoken several times on the phone and had great conversations. He was smart and funny and all of those things men generally aren't these days. Surely he would understand that flowers don't have to mean something sinister.

He did call, about an hour after the roses arrived. I was out walking the dog and came home to find the message light blinking on my answering machine.

"Hi," said his voice when I hit the button. "Thanks so much for the flowers. They're really, um, nice. Look, about Friday. I guess I should have explained that I'm, um, not really ready to date anyone seriously."

It went on, but we needn't get into the grisly details. Suffice it to say, it was not a joyous moment and it involved the phrase "still be friends."

That Friday, instead of going out with my would-be beau, I went out with Anna and Jackson. "You win," I said as soon as we sat down. I told them what had happened.

"See," said Anna jadedly when I was finished. "It never works. You scared him."

"You should have just sent him E-mail saying you wanted to savage him if it was convenient," suggested Jackson. "That's more to the point."

Before I could argue, the waitress appeared at our table, interrupting our discussion. "Here you go," she said, setting down a votive candle. "Especially for my favorite customers."

She smiled at us and left. As she walked away, I picked up the candle.

"And just what's this supposed to mean?" I said, blowing it out. "I bet she just wants a bigger tip"

"See," said Anna, patting me on the back. "Now you're catching on."

What a Tangled Web

Every time I turn on the television lately there's someone complaining about smut on the Internet and how it's infecting the minds of innocent children. I had no idea the young people of America were under siege, but I gather from the frequency with which the issue crops up on shows from *Oprah* to CNN programs that it concerns a great number of folks. These people all speak emphatically about how easy it is for children to just turn a computer on and within minutes find themselves smack in the middle of a veritable orgy. According to them, all manner of wickedness is available at the click of a mouse: lesbianism, dildos, incest, S/M, kiddie porn. Bestiality is a favorite bugaboo; every single person I've heard expounding on this subject has mentioned it about 56 times, as though images of housewives doing it with cocker spaniels are flooding kindergartens everywhere.

Apparently this outcry started because some kids in New York (where else) went to the New York Public Library and used a reference computer to download beaver shots. Now, I used to live in New York, and I've done a lot of research at that very same library. On a good day I was lucky if I could find a magazine I needed. More often I spent my time there avoiding the shifty-eyed men who liked to hide in the stacks and show unsuspecting passers-by their unruly members. The copiers never worked. The librarians were surly. The chairs were stained with suspiciously sticky fluids. And they're worried about a couple of kids finding *Playboy* on the Net?

But someone is worried. Many someones. They're so worried that they want to ban all pornography from the electronic highways so that no unsuspecting child, attempting to find the *Sesame Street* home page or the *Teletubbies* fan club, stumbles across pictures of men dressed in leather boinking one another in the behind. To prevent such tragedies, these folks want immediate legislation to protect, yes, that old favorite of panic-stricken conservatives everywhere—family values.

This topic interests me for several reasons. For one thing, I write a lot of books for young people, so I like to think that I have at least a passing interest in what they're up to these days. As it so happens, I've also written and edited a number of pornographic books. While the two interests have never before crossed in any way, I find the whole notion of dirty words and pictures being harmful an interesting one. Add to this my infinite fascination with the stupidity of human beings, especially those who think the government Knows What's Right for Everyone, and this whole topic is greatly appealing to me. So I decided to find out for myself what the fuss was all about.

I will admit right up front that I am not a particularly adept Web surfer. Decidedly Luddite in my approach to technology, I have only the most basic setup. My elderly computer will grudgingly allow me to connect to the various pages I urge it toward, but it moans about it the whole time. And frequently, in the middle of transmission, it will give up entirely and refuse to do anything at all. So my exploration of the wonderful world of the Internet has been limited primarily to searching for pages with my name on them, and I even gave that up after I discovered myself listed on the home page of a right-wing Christian group who found my book *100 Questions*

& Answers about AIDS to be antifamily and pro–homo-sexual agenda.

Still, if mere children can do it, surely I, a reasonably intelligent adult, can do it too. Especially if, as these self-proclaimed pro-family people keep insisting, perverted Web sites practically suck unsuspecting users in the minute you log on. So I turned on the computer and prepared to enter the world of sin. I fully expected that within seconds I would be gazing upon all sorts of things that would have me blushing and pulling down the blinds.

Since bestiality is such a recurring theme of this debate, I decided to start there. I went to my search engine, typed in the word, and waited. Sure enough, it came back with 236 different sites that claimed to be devoted to this sordid fetish. I clicked on the first one and held my breath.

I could have held it forever with no effect, because the site was unreachable. As were 95% of the others I tried. But some did work, and my computer happily took me to them. Unfortunately, they were about as interesting, and as lurid, as a speech at the Republican Convention. Most were academic sites talking about things like adolescent fascination with goats and the manhood ceremonies of some tribe in South America involving llamas and a paddle. One did feature a man's badly rhyming love poem to a poodle he once had but, alas, it was unillustrated.

I tried again. This time I typed in "bondage." I was awarded with a jackpot of 785 sites to choose from. But again I was disappointed. Most of the sites turned out to be unavailable. Others were simply listings of bondage clubs throughout the United States which, while helpful, were not especially titillating. One did show a lovely photo of a woman spanking a man dressed in a schoolgirl uniform and sprawled across her knee, but it was hardly enough to get crazy over.

All in all, I spent six hours online attempting to find some kind—any kind—of pornography. Maybe I was doing it wrong. Maybe I'm just hopelessly stupid. Whatever the case, I found nary a hint of skin. Sure, I found a couple of sites promising hot photos, live sex, nasty girls and boys, and every conceivable kind of perversion. But even when I could get to them, I never got past the first page. After tempting me with some blurry R-rated pictures and having me click a button promising to God that I was over 18 years of age and thought that pornography was in no way detrimental to the health of my community, they quickly doused any lusting thoughts I might have had—they all demanded credit card payment before putting out.

Now, I sincerely doubt there are hordes of seven-year-olds out there with their very own Visa cards. If they do have them and are responsible for paying off the balances, then as far as I'm concerned they deserve to look at all the porn they want to. And if their parents are stupid enough to loan them their cards, then they should just shut up about it. Any kid that spoiled isn't going to be ruined any further by looking at a few wienies. In fact, it will probably do him some good.

I admit my experiment was less than comprehensive in scope. I'm sure there is a lot of weird stuff out there. And maybe some kids are finding ways to get their hands on it. If they are, I wish they'd come over and show me how to find it. Anyway, what the hell if they are. When I was 12 I used to steal *Playgirl* from the Reader's Island at the mall, and I haven't gone on a mad raping and pillaging spree. Yet. Besides, there are a lot worse things they could be finding—like the Kathie Lee Gifford Home Page. Now that's sick.

I Wish Me a
Merry Christmas

When I was a kid, I loved Christmas. In fact, it was the highlight of my entire year, the day that all the rest led up to. I started looking forward to it sometime in September, when the air first grew cooler and the leaves began their gradual descent into drifts of gold and orange. For me, this signaled the beginning of the Holiday Bowl, the series of evenly spaced celebrations culminating in the Big Day.

First came my birthday, followed by Halloween and then Thanksgiving. Each of these minor days had its own delights, and each made the anticipation mount just that much more. But in the end they were merely precursors to the magical allure of the Yuletide season, warm-ups for the big game. Like a football fanatic glued to the television as game after game rolled on in preparation for the Super Bowl, I saw each passing holiday as another step bringing me closer to December 25.

The source of all of this joy was, of course, gifts. More precisely, it was the anticipation of receiving gifts, preferably in vast quantities. My fervently religious mother tried her best to remind me that the true purpose of the holiday was to celebrate the birth of Jesus, but I knew better. Nobody deserved a birthday party this big. There had to be something else going on to make everyone run around like crazy trimming trees, singing carols, and being nice to one another for an entire month or so. Even the Christ child, I was sure, lay in the manger tolerating all the adoration of the heavenly host only because he knew full well that three very wealthy men were headed his way loaded down with piles of loot.

The centerpiece of my Christmas season excitement was the marvelous Sears Wish Book, a catalog of approximately the same weight and importance as the Gutenberg Bible. Every fall it arrived in the mailbox, heralding the official start of my holiday celebration. The day it came was a special one indeed. Snatching it up, I feverishly ripped away the paper wrapping and held the catalog to my face. It had a distinctive scent I can recall vividly even to this day—a mixture of ink, paper, and glue headier than any sheet of freshly baked cookies or newly cut pine garland. Opening it up and pressing my nose into the crease between the pages, I would inhale the delicious aroma until, dizzy, I was forced to sit quietly for a few moments while my head cleared.

From that point on, the quest for gifts began in earnest. Taking the Wish Book up to my room, I pored over it endlessly, making very careful lists of all of the items I wanted. Each page was meticulously combed over for rare and fascinating things I just had to find under the tree on Christmas morning: action figures complete with their assorted vehicles and paraphernalia, remote-control airplanes, board games of all sorts, gumball machines, a record player. It was like having my own personal toy store. Every new treasure I came across went onto the list, until I had a notebook filled with wishes culled from the register of fine items available at our local Sears store.

Over the weeks preceding Christmas, this list went through numerous revisions as my wants and desires changed. I knew I couldn't have *everything,* so I worked and reworked the list until it contained approximately

127 essential items. But no matter how many times it was rewritten, I always had it completed shortly after Thanksgiving, when I solemnly presented it to my parents and informed them that my life would be utterly bereft should I not receive the gifts so thoughtfully outlined (with catalog numbers included) to make the holiday shopping chore swift and efficient. Young though I was, I had my suspicions that even if Santa did exist, he apparently hired my parents to do all of his purchasing for him, and I wasn't taking any chances.

Finished with this weighty duty, I was then free to jump headlong into the rest of the holiday activities—stringing popcorn with glee, sledding down the hill behind the house until the melting snow seeped into my snowsuit, laughing as Charlie Brown and the gang danced around the littlest tree. But through it all the vision of Christmas morning and the unwrapping of my gifts filled my head like a guiding star. I even practiced feigning surprise, so that in any photos taken on the glorious day my expression would appear both spontaneous and heartfelt.

Each Christmas Eve, my mother dragged us all to church for the requisite nod to the religious aspects of the holiday. Ever mindful of the thin line that separated Good Boys from Bad Boys on the Naughty/Nice List, I sat piously, mouthing the words to "O, Holy Night" while I thought ahead to the electric race cars with hand-held controls I was sure awaited me the next morning. Later at home, I lay in bed, tossing and turning as I tried fruitlessly to fall asleep. My mind raced breathlessly as I pictured over and over again that magical moment I knew would occur sometime as I slept, when the barren tree standing in the silent living room would suddenly bloom with gaily wrapped packages, all with my name written on their tags. Eventually, of course, I would fall into a deep, expectant slumber.

Then, oh, the glory of Christmas morning and that first opening of the eyes, when suddenly the long-awaited moment had arrived. Leaping from my bed, I would rush down the stairs to the living room, falling upon the presents like a hungry jackal on a wounded wildebeest. I showed no mercy as I shredded paper and ribbon to see what lay beneath. As each item from my list was duly noted, I cast it aside and reached for the next box. It was generally all over in about 20 minutes, after which I would lie on the floor, looking up at the ceiling with my assorted bounty piled high around me, and begin to plan for the next year.

Such were the first of my Christmases. They were happy times, filled with laughter and smiles, giggles and shrieks of delight. As each December rolled around and a new Wish Book materialized, I immersed myself in its glow, oblivious to the fact that disaster was just around the corner. Alas, like Cinderella finding that her magical ball was not to last forever, my Yuletide nirvana came crashing down on December 25, 1977, the year I was nine. For that was the Year of Practical Presents, the cursed day when all of my sugarplum Christmas mornings would turn, with one stroke of the clock, into a big, boring pumpkin. It would mark the end of my childhood and the beginning of an aversion to Christmas that lingers like a bitter taste in my mouth to this very day.

Things began normally enough. The Wish Book arrived, right on schedule, and I immediately began to make plans for what I hoped would be the best holiday season ever. I distinctly recall that that year's list featured, among other indispensable items, an entire set of *Star Wars* action figures, a beanbag chair, a telescope, Sea Monkeys, a Huffy mountain bike, several kinds of Hot Wheels, and roller skates, which although decidedly a summer item were nonetheless crucial to my having a successful Christmas. This list I dutifully wrote up and handed to my parents well in advance of the season. I was careful not to be too greedy and only requested gifts of utmost importance.

I suspected nothing. Sure, the old animated Christmas specials were getting a little tired, but I still thrilled to the antics of Heatmeiser and Coldmeiser in *The Year Without a Santa Claus* and chortled with enthusiasm along with the rest of the family at Rudolph's shiny nose. And while I'd begun to weary of the chirpy sing-along sound of the *Mitch Miller Christmas Album,* I still joined in on "We Wish You a Merry Christmas," my heart filled with good will toward men as I thought of all the great joys awaiting me at the end of it all. It was a year like any other year, filled with innocent expectation and hope.

Imagine my horror, then, when on Christmas morning I tore the wrapping off the first box and discovered beneath it not the chemistry set with microscope I'd expected, but a plain old blue sweater. I took a deep breath to calm myself. Having encountered such unexpected, unpleasant gifts in the past, I knew from experience that they sometimes were slipped in among the real presents by grandparents and other well-meaning relations who simply didn't know any better. While disappointing, the best thing to do was to move on quickly and pick up the thread of joy before the whole thing unraveled. I snatched up another box.

That one contained three pairs of socks, two pairs of underwear, and a package of undershirts. All white. Things were looking grim indeed. Filled with growing panic, I rabidly clawed through the remaining presents, unearthing two pairs of jeans, a sweatshirt, one pair of plaid flannel pajamas, and a turtleneck sweater. No action figures. No beanbag chair. Definitely no telescope. I was distraught.

"Do you like your gifts?" my mother asked, beaming at me over her mug of coffee. "Santa must have known you needed new clothes this year."

I was speechless. Where was the air rifle? Where were the lawn darts? Where was the fully poseable G.I. Joe with jeep and parachute set? Either someone was playing a cruel joke or this was the worst Christmas ever. In a matter of minutes, my world had been turned upside down. Not only did I now have to fully accept that Santa had been replaced by my mother, but I was dealt the harsher blow of having to parade around in the symbols of her betrayal. "Try them on," she said cheerfully, holding up some green corduroy pants. "Let's see how they look."

Suffice it to say that life was not merry and gay for me that year. And things did not improve in subsequent years, which brought such useful gifts as weatherproof boots, a globe, several ties, and an entire set of Tom Swift novels, which apparently my father had enjoyed immensely as a young boy. As the years rolled on and the gifts became less and less thrilling, I realized that the time of really cool Christmas presents was over. On my 13th Christmas, gazing down on the second wallet I'd unearthed after opening only four gifts, I suddenly knew that adulthood had little to do with getting a driver's license or discovering the joys of masturbation. No, becoming a man meant something much crueler: It meant getting socks for Christmas.

Since then Christmas has become a time of great disappointment for me. While I try to muster some enthusiasm for it each year, it gets harder and harder as the accumulated weight of endless pairs of socks crushes my spirit like a hammer to the heart. I no longer like even the thought of gifts, because it only reopens the harsh wounds of the lessons I learned in my youth. I don't dare even hope that maybe this year things will be different, because I couldn't stand the pain of finding they won't.

For years I tried dutifully to go through with it all, attempting to exorcise the Spirit of Crappy Christmas Presents through aggressive merrymaking. Each year around Thanksgiving I would draw up lists of my friends and loved ones and try to think of unusual, fascinating gifts that would make them cry out with joy on opening the boxes. I searched out-of-the-way shops for things that obviously hadn't been picked up during a last-minute scramble through the bins at the local drugstore. I tried to find quirky surprises to match equally peculiar personalities. But it never worked out. Inevitably, after 16 hours of attempting to find something no one else had thought of, I'd end up in the Macy's Cellar, trying to estimate the glove sizes of everyone I knew.

So after years of failed attempts, I have resolved that I will no longer try. This year I am sending around a short note to everyone who might expect a present from me, explaining that rather than waste money buying things no one really wants, I am going to donate the cash to a worthy cause. I am not telling them that the cause is me and that I'm using what I'll save on their gifts to take a week's vacation on a little island where I can blissfully lie in the sun while someone brings me fruit drinks and trashy novels and a hunky masseur named Ben rubs the years of disappointment from my weary muscles. On Christmas Day, while all over the world people open boxes to find yet more socks, I will look out from behind my sunglasses and smile. Hoisting my frothy drink to the sky, I will laugh defiantly and fling myself into Ben's waiting arms.

Bah, humbug, indeed. At least I know I'm getting something I like. But if you really want a gift, I think I still have a few pairs of gloves left over from last year. What size do you take again?

Part Two
Us and Them

My Contract
on America: A Fantasy

I'm thinking of going on a killing spree.

Don't worry. I'm not going to do it right this minute or anything. I still have a little bit of planning left to do. And if you want to know the truth, the entire plan is actually pretty shaky, primarily because it hinges upon my contracting a fatal disease. And not just me, but my friend Katherine too. See, Katherine and I have decided that if we ever discover that we have some decidedly deadly disease (we use inoperable brain cancer in our scenario, but you may substitute anything you like) we are going to go out in a blaze of glory by taking some key people along with us.

By key people we mean people who, in our opinion, deserve to die because they just don't get it. This group consists primarily of congresspeople, religious leaders, and others with antigay, antiwoman, anti–health care, and generally stupid views. Stupid, just for the record, means those we disagree with. We are hardly impartial, and we freely admit that. On days when we're really crabby or when we accidentally happen to catch a glimpse of a newspaper, we also include on the list certain world leaders who will go unnamed and Catholic figureheads who may or may not be Cardinal John O'Connor.

The way we figure it, the plan is foolproof. Once a weapon is secured—which can be readily accomplished by giving any third grader in New York $25—the actual act of assassination is relatively easy. The people who really deserve to die generally do not adopt adequate protection for such emergencies, as they can't imagine that anyone would not be impressed by their ability to always be right. Eliminating them is just a matter of being in the right place at the right time. With a little luck we would probably be able to pick off several morons in the space of a couple of days or, if we concentrate on the Capitol Hill area of Washington, even a few hours. Even in the worst-case scenario, the chances are that we could take out at least one jerk—say, just for the sake of argument, a certain senator from North Carolina—before anyone got suspicious. The way we see it, bagging even one member of the idiot brigade would make it worthwhile, and we could then die knowing our lives had been fraught with purpose.

Now ordinarily, an undertaking such as the one we propose would be foolhardy at best. After all, in America you can't just kill someone and get away with it, unless, of course, you happen to be a highly popular sports figure or you chose as your victim someone from a minority group, meaning anyone who is not a heterosexual white male. In those instances, you can probably rest easy, knowing that the people in charge of investigating such things—notably heterosexual white males—will not feel endangered in the least and will probably leave you alone. But Katherine and I are not particularly well-known in the sports world. And while some of our targets might come from other groups, the majority would be white, male, and heterosexual. This makes it slightly more risky than it might otherwise be, especially for Katherine, since white, heterosexual males do not take at all kindly to being shot at by persons with vaginas, as they somehow believe it shows flagrant disrespect for the supremacy of the penis.

That's where the fatal illness comes into play. While the eradication of stupidity is always a good idea, there's no point in engaging in it at the expense of your own happiness. We are hardly selfless martyrs to the cause. But being practical people, Katherine and I agree that if we're going to die anyway, we might as well have fun on the way out. After all, where is the joy in sitting around waiting to go when you could be outside getting some fresh air and meeting new people?

Besides, consider if you will the possible endings to our plan. If we are killed while carrying out our idea, then it's all over with one quick shot to the heart by a skilled SWAT team member. In that case the police look foolish for offing terminally ill people and we depart this life relatively easily. Surely a fast death after ridding the world of a little bit of evil is preferable to lingering around uselessly and racking up huge hospital bills that would go unpaid after our deaths. Even someone like Pat Buchanan would have to admire our thoughtfulness, unless—and I'm not saying for certain that his name is or is not on our list—he happens to be one of the people we get to first, in which event he would likely have a less cheerful outlook on the whole thing. We would also, I'm sure, gain instant sainthood among oppressed peoples everywhere. Perhaps we would even get an alternative rock band named after us, which would be worth any small amount of suffering we might endure.

But before we go getting all excited, let's look at the other option. If, instead of becoming heroic victims of the despotic white patriarchy, we are merely captured and punished, in all likelihood we'd spend our remaining days in a facility where we were fed, clothed, and exercised regularly—at no expense to us. After years of living as freelancers with no health care and more than a passing acquaintance with ramen and Woolworth's white sales, even the barren cells of Sing Sing would seem to us to be the Ritz-Carlton. Not only that, but we'd be sure to be extremely popular with the other inmates, who tend not to be inordinately fond of the sort of people who make up our intended targets.

Of the two most likely options, I think I prefer death, if only because I dislike the idea of having to spend so much time with other people and because I do not give good sound bites when interviewed. However, I am open to all the possibilities, and if a movie is made, I would just like it noted that I think George Clooney would make a wonderful me. Katherine casts her vote for Dianne Wiest.

Mind you, these two possible outcomes assume that capture, dead or alive, is a foregone conclusion. But really, there's no reason at all why things shouldn't go off without a hitch. In that case we would be left to continue our merry death dance until we were too tired or bored to go on. A sort of demented Thelma and Louise, we would roll across America ridding the world of people who make life annoying, although in our version no one knows who we really are because we look like tourists from Connecticut and drive a very old Toyota. Blending in easily, we would remain undercover as long as possible, although we both agree that the whole thing wouldn't be half as much fun if it had to be carried out anonymously. After all, while we do think there is a generous amount of concern for the public good in our plan, primarily we just want to make ourselves feel better about our lives, and scaring the crap out of the miserable little bastards is a good start.

More than a few people are appalled by our annihilation fantasy, feigning politically correct liberal shock at the mere suggestion of murdering another human being, no matter how vile she or he may be. These gentle souls believe in the power of the political system and in the strength of voting. They insist that a voice raised in protest says more than a dozen stones thrown in anger. "Remember Gandhi," they cry, renewing their memberships in the Human Rights Campaign and trundling off to recycle their bottles.

To those people we say: Get out of our way.

Really, if we're honest about it, how many of us would be at all mournful to hear that someone like, say, Senator Helms had been murdered by vigilantes or even by people who merely found the activity amusing? When it comes down to it, there's a thin line between finding something acceptable when other people do it for us and doing it ourselves because we're tired of waiting. All it takes is a willingness to cross that line, a state easily reached simply by watching the latest congressional hearings regarding gay marriage on CNN, where yet more heterosexual white men debate whether or not they should *give* us equal rights under the law. Whether or not you favor gay marriage (and I don't favor marriage of any kind), listening to these guys talk about our lives as if they have any clue about them is infuriating. And who has time to wait for them to die? When you think about it, isn't our plan a lot more effective than pledging another $50 to PBS or plastering a Greenpeace sticker on the Subaru?

Actually, I'm surprised that no one else has thought of this. Katherine and I were sure that some clever person in ACT UP would have done it years ago, and we briefly thought about copyrighting our idea before it could be co-opted by other activists far more pissed off or motivated than ourselves. After all, if they can make a condom fit over Jesse Helms's house, surely they can figure out how to work a handgun. Then there are the women fed up with inadequate breast cancer research, people who suffer from easily treated illnesses because of unaffordable health care, victims of the tobacco industry and its lobby, and really any people with any sense at all who find themselves in the position of having limited time left, lots of pent-up energy, and no desire whatsoever to get in touch with their anger through interpretive dance.

Ideally, I suppose, the most impressive thing to do would be to marshal all of these folks into one big army. The problem with that, of course, is that a militia of the dying and angry is hard to organize effectively. Debilitating illnesses develop at different rates, and it would be no small feat to get everyone ready to go on the same day, which we see as being crucial to a successful national operation. That's why we think it's better to work in small teams of two or three. Large groups are easily caught or divided, which can ruin things for everyone, and lone gunmen are too risky, tending to be too flashy at the last minute and thus proving unreliable. Besides, in the later stages of illness it's sometimes difficult to aim steadily, and a partner can provide helpful suggestions, not to mention drive a getaway car.

In the end, it's all theoretical anyway. As I said, most likely neither Katherine nor I will ever be in a position where we actually have a chance to set our operation in motion. And if we did, I'm sure we'd have better things to worry about than a handful of idiot heterosexual white men trying to keep their gasping vision of a perfect world alive for another day. But I admit that it's nice to think about. Sometimes when I see another hatemonger spewing forth about protecting family values or whining about how straight people have it so rough in this country, I close my eyes and imagine how he (or she) would look standing in his (or her) driveway, staring with bemused surprise at the gun in my hand. In my mind, I gleefully pull the trigger and hop into the convertible as he (or she) ceases to irritate me. Katherine steps on the gas, and we roar off accompanied by the sounds of Melissa Etheridge blasting from the stereo.

Holy Ghost in the Machine

My CD player has been possessed by the religious right.

For years it worked just fine, opening its obedient little mouth and happily swallowing and then spewing forth whatever I put into it, no matter how offensive. All it took was a simple push of a button and the house would fill with the sounds of everything from ABBA to Marilyn Manson, Beethoven to Garbage.

But no more. Someone's gotten to it, and I think I know who. It all started several weeks ago, when I dropped *Closet Classics Vol. 1* (a sampler of acts on Boy George's More Protein record label) into the player and settled in to enjoy myself. I waited for the opening track—E-Zee Possee's infectious queer club anthem "Everything Starts with an 'E'"—to come blasting from the speakers. It was time to party.

But instead all I heard was a feeble little series of clicks, like a pair of press-on nails being drummed across a Formica countertop by a disapproving Sunday School teacher faced with a child who cannot for the life of him remember what comes after Jeremiah in the order of the books of the Bible. Click-click-click, click-click-click.

I ejected the CD and cleaned it, innocently suspecting that dirt, or maybe even some stray drops of lube, was causing the problem. Then back into the player it went.

Again the click-click-click trickled from the speakers like lukewarm water.

I took the CD into my roommate's office and tried it in his stereo. It played just fine. Using scientific logic, I decided that my CD player's internal workings must be at fault. Out came the tool set. Off went the metal casing of the player. Dog hair was evacuated. Lenses were cleaned. Everything was made as sterile as the day it came off the assembly line.

I put it all back together again, then once more laid E-Zee Possee to rest in the plastic cradle of the CD changer. Again I hit the play button. And again I heard nothing but that irritating click-click-click.

For whatever reason, my CD player was steadfastly refusing to play a disc it had played hundreds of times before with no complaint. Determined to root out the cause of the problem, I found my roommate's copy of *Closet Classics* and put it in my player. If something was wrong with just my copy, that would explain everything. But if the player refused to give voice to his copy as well, then something more sinister was going on.

I hit play and held my breath. After whirring for a few seconds as it always does, my player seemed on the verge of giving in. But then, perhaps sensing that it was being tricked, it began anew with the dreaded click-click-click. This time I saw in my mind a vision of a pious minister shaking his head and clucking at the sins of the congregation. The CD spun around helplessly, its underside scanned and rejected by the condemning red eye of the self-righteous laser.

Normally I would just assume that something technological had gone awry with my wayward piece of audio electronics. But I have a history of music-related confrontations stemming back to my childhood, and I was beginning to have a strong suspicion that something from my youth had come back to haunt me.

I grew up with a strict Baptist mother for whom rock music was the voice of Satan himself. When I was very young, the only nonclassical music heard in our home was that of cowboy crooner Marty Robbins, whom my father loved, and the trilling religious harmonies of the Bill Gaither Trio. Of course, we were living in the middle of Africa at the time, and it wasn't as if popular music radio stations were plentiful. Even the state-run television channel only showed two programs—the daily news and *Mighty Mouse* cartoons, and both were in French.

But when we returned stateside, we discovered the '70s in full swing. Music had become the defining influence on society, and my sisters, being a decade older than me, took to it like the culture-starved teenagers they in fact were. Thus began the first round in the holy war my mother waged against our listening options.

My eldest sister fulfilled her musical destiny by becoming obsessed with Elvis to the exclusion of all other music. This for some reason was tolerated by my mother, probably because by that stage of his career Presley was too old and fat to incite dangerous levels of rebellion. Besides, I think she secretly harbored her own schoolgirl crush on the King and couldn't bear to deny her daughter the same opportunity.

But my other sister was a problem. Anxious to do anything that would send my mother into a fury, she promptly latched on to the likes of Jethro Tull and Black Sabbath. Locking herself in her room, she would play these records just loudly enough so that my mother would know what she was up to and come running downstairs to bang on the bedroom door, threatening to cut off Karen's allowance if she didn't pluck the needle from the turntable immediately.

So there I was, caught in the middle. As I was still at an age where I thought listening to things like the sound track from Disney's *The Rescuers* was fun, my own musical tastes did not pose an immediate threat to my relationship with my mother. I had a tinny little record player in my bedroom, and when not listening to Christian recordings such as *Little Miss Teardrop* or *Sing-a-Long for Jesus,* I delighted myself with things like Sterling Holloway reading *Winnie-the-Pooh* and a collection of tunes called *Alley Cat and Chicken Fat.* This peculiar record contained songs like "On Top of Spaghetti," "Great Green Gobs of Greasy Grimy Gopher Guts," and, inexplicably, "Mrs. Brown You've Got a Lovely Daughter." It was in questionable taste, but my mother tolerated it, probably because next to Jethro Tull's *Aqualung* it was positively uplifting.

As the years went by, I did manage to amass a larger collection of records, composed primarily of 45s my sisters purchased when they were popular and then, having grown weary of them, passed along to me. My mother examined each new addition carefully before allowing me to play it, searching the lyrics for anything that might be unseemly. Thus, by the time I was eight or nine, I had a small shelf of vinyl made up of Elton John's "Crocodile Rock," The Archies' "Sugar Sugar," Elvis's "In the Ghetto," and Linda Ronstadt's "Silver Threads and Golden Needles." For a brief time I had enjoyed a copy of Mouth & Macneal's "How Do You Do?" but that ended when my mother decided that the nonsense syllables of the chorus "and then we can mnah-mnah" must be some kind of secret code for an unseemly act, and she took it away.

The records I was allowed to have I listened to endlessly, feeling quite sophisticated indeed, and my mother was content with the fact that she had managed to keep my ears unpolluted by the sounds of harsher fare. Unfortunately for her, however, I did not always remain in my room. I did from time to time venture out into the world. I even mingled with children whose parents found nothing wrong with rock music. One of these was my best friend, Stephanie, whose father had not only purchased her an entire stereo system, but had loaded her up with records ranging from Blondie's *Parallel Lines* to the Captain and Tennille's *Love Will Keep Us Together*. These we listened to with great abandon, dancing around Stephanie's Holly Hobbie bedroom until we were dizzy.

Our favorite group of all was Kiss, who were then at the height of their popularity. We found them absolutely mesmerizing, and dedicated ourselves to following their every move in magazines like *Tiger Beat* and *16*. This was a crucial tactical error on my part, because the religious crowd my mother ran in had already latched on to Kiss as the elite color guard of the devil's personal troops. They announced that, in fact, the very name Kiss stood for Kings In Satan's Service and that the Kiss fan club, called the Army, was nothing more than a recruitment tool for ushering young people straight into the ranks of hell's foot soldiers.

While I couldn't be caught with even a single Kiss trading card, Stephanie could have all of the Kiss merchandise she wanted. Her room became a shrine to our gods, filled with Kiss posters, Kiss puzzles, Kiss dolls, and Kiss board games. Whenever I could, I would sneak over to her house and we would worship our heroes. Using wash-off Magic Markers, we painted our faces to match those of our favorite Kiss member, drummer Peter Criss. With our drawn-on cat eyes and whiskers, we pounded imaginary drum sets while Peter played, until it was time for dinner and I had to scrub the marks of my betrayal away in Stephanie's bathroom before scampering home to dinner.

Things fell apart the day I convinced Stephanie to let me borrow her copy of Kiss's *Alive II*. I took it home and, thinking my mother was out shopping, put it on. She went into hysterics when she walked into my bedroom and caught me singing "Calling Dr. Love" into my hairbrush. Only repeated washings of my mouth with Ivory soap could, in her opinion, rid me of the lingering stain caused by those lyrics. It was the first volley in what would escalate into an all-out war.

As I grew older and entered my teens, things got worse. I loved music, and listened to it as much as I could. My mother was as appalled as I was excited, and daily we entered the musical arena and battled it out. I played Journey's *Departure* over and over, and she countered by throwing out my REO Speedwagon album when I was at school. She frequently left books about the evil possibilities of rock music in my room. From these I learned that Stevie Nicks was the devil's willing whore and that anyone who even thought about playing a Jefferson Starship record might as well just buy a first-class ticket to the burning place. When I defied her and went to a Prince concert, she didn't speak to me for a week.

I thought that when I went away to college my musical tribulations would be over. But my mother took care of that by making sure I attended a Bible college. There I found that the war between religion and rock music could become even more heated. Not an hour after my arrival at the dorm, my roommate took one look at my vast tape collection and announced that he couldn't live with me because anyone who willingly subjected himself to groups as spiritually poisonous as Missing Persons and Katrina and the Waves was not a suitable living companion.

But this was nothing compared to the infamous Amy Grant Scandal that rocked the very foundations of Christian homes everywhere. For a long time Amy had been a favorite of religious listeners. She was wholesome. She had a nice voice. She provided a midpoint between the secular and the sacred. We were actually encouraged to listen to her, and on more than one occasion, my school had invited her to perform concerts and no one raised a fuss.

But then Amy released her 1985 album *Unguarded.* While the lyrics were still about Jesus and redemption, the music featured electric guitars and forceful drumming. Even worse, Amy appeared on the cover wearing a sporty leopard-print jacket. Christian parents, who heretofore had adored Amy, became suspicious that she was becoming just a little too much like Mick Jagger. When two of the songs from the record were used on the sound track to *Miami Vice,* warning flags went up around the country.

Things might have ironed themselves out. But then Amy did the unforgivable. In an interview in the Christian teen magazine *Campus Life,* Amy told the interviewer that she "got horny like everyone else." That did it. Overnight we were forbidden to listen to this harlot in heat, who not only wore leopard print but actually admitted to sometimes becoming moist. It was the end of Christian pop music as we knew it, and once again we were told that only the great hymns of the faith were suitable for our impressionable ears.

I hadn't thought about the Amy Grant fiasco or my mother's antirock mania for years. But now my CD player was acting out, and I knew there must be a reason. Somehow I thought that maybe, just maybe, it was all connected to the religious censors of my past. After all, they have been on the warpath again about the detrimental effects of rock music. And I wouldn't be at all surprised if my mother gave them my address.

I decided to experiment. Replacing *Closet Classics* with a pre-*Unguarded* Amy Grant CD I still had in my collection, I tried again. This time the CD player had no hesitation, filling the room with Amy's bland but harmless crooning. Now I knew I was on to something.

For the next hour I tried various discs, noting the machine's response to each one. It was perfectly happy to play Bach, Bob Dylan's conversion-themed *Slow Train Coming,* and anything by Enya. Oddly, it also had no issues with Wynonna. But it flat-out balked at Dylan's earlier *Blood on the Tracks,* Phranc's *Goofyfoot,* and the more flamboyant Mozart piano concertos. When I tried to fool it by putting Donna Summer's *Greatest Hits* in the five-disc tray along with a Vienna Boys Choir album, Patrick Stewart's narration of *Peter and the Wolf,* a Mitch Miller Christmas collection, and the *Sound of Music* sound track and using the shuffle function, it behaved perfectly until "MacArthur Park" came on, at which point it spat the disc, *Exorcist*-like, onto the floor.

That was all the proof I needed. I yanked the power cord out of the wall and watched as the CD player's little red electronic eyes closed for the last time. I have since purchased a new one, one which happily, even drunkenly, plays "Everything Starts with an 'E'" whenever I ask it to. My friends all say I'm paranoid to think that the Bible thumpers had anything to do with this. Maybe they're right. But I'm still not convinced that the Crazy Christers aren't somehow infiltrating my home electronics through the power lines. Last night I turned on the television to lust after the hunky Australian rugby players on ESPN, and for some reason every single channel I flipped to was showing *Touched by an Angel.*

Us and Them

It's the day after Ellen came out to the world in a blaze of media glory. Roger, my black Lab, and I are enjoying our daily early-morning romp with his play group at the park. The dogs are chasing sticks, balls, and one another. The rest of us are, of course, talking about "The Show."

"There's something I just don't understand about lesbians," says Jeff (straight, outdoorsy, likes girls who can hike).

"What's that?" I ask.

"I have this friend," he says. "I always knew she was a lesbian, and that was cool. I mean, I don't care. Then yesterday she said she was bringing her girlfriend over. So she comes in the house, and she's with this guy. Only after a couple of minutes I realize it's not a guy, it's a really mannish woman."

"So what don't you get?" I say.

"Well, if she doesn't like men, why would she be with a woman who looks like one? She's really beautiful and girly-looking, and this girlfriend looks like Ed over at the Texaco station."

Jeff's dog, Rumpus, is trying to mount Roger, who growls and pins him to the ground. I toss a tennis ball at them, and they break it up, both going after the ball with tails wagging.

"They're a butch-femme couple," I tell him.

"Butch-femme?" he says, confused. "What's that?"

I glance over at my friend Megan (dyke, very funny, pierced tongue). She rolls her eyes. Her dog, k.d., a hyperactive pug, is fervently courting a female husky, her tiny nose buried in the husky's crotch from below.

"Sometimes very feminine-looking lesbians pair up with more…mannish…lesbians," I say to Jeff, trying to make it as simple as possible. "Get it? Femmes and butches."

Jeff nods. "OK," he says. "But why?"

"Why not?" says Megan. "They're just attracted to each other. People like different things."

He still isn't getting it. "But if they don't like men…" he says.

"It's not about not liking men," says Megan curtly. "It's about not liking penises."

"Actually," I say, seeing that Jeff is about to start in on penis-hating dykes, "it's about liking vaginas."

"Or licking vaginas," adds Megan thoughtfully.

"That I understand," says Jeff. "But if you want to be with women, why not be with women? You know, real women."

"With long hair and nails and makeup?" I say.

"Exactly," says Jeff. "I mean, like why would Laura Dern be interested in Ellen? I didn't buy it at all."

"That's why you don't have a girlfriend," says Megan, clearly irritated.

"Would *you* sleep with Ellen?" Jeff asks her.

"No," Megan admits. "But I'd definitely sleep with Laura Dern."

"Why wouldn't you sleep with Ellen?" I ask her.

"I don't know," Megan says. "She seems like she'd be too uptight. And that hair. Now, Demi Moore, she's hot."

"She's not gay," says Jeff. "She's married to Bruce Willis."

I look at Megan and get a wicked idea. "But Bruce is gay," I tell Jeff. "Everyone knows that. They're just married so no one will suspect."

Jeff's mouth drops open. "He is not," he says. "He can't be."

"It's true," says Megan, managing, unlike Oprah during Ellen's coming-out, to keep a straight face. "Someone I know slept with him once."

Jeff is in shock at the idea of superbutch Bruce being queer. "Who else is gay?" he asks, like I have the secret list in my pocket.

"Oh, lots of people," I say casually. "You'd be surprised."

"Bruce Willis," says Jeff. "Wow."

At that moment we're interrupted by the arrival of Nick, another dog park regular. Nick is a big jocky type, and I've lusted after him ever since he started coming with his rottweiler, who is named after boxing champ Oscar de la Hoya. Oscar adores me and immediately jumps up and starts licking my face. I close my eyes and pretend he's Nick.

"Hey," says Nick. "What's up?"

"They're telling me who's gay," Jeff says. "Did you know Bruce Willis is a fag?"

"Get out," Nick says. "How would you guys know who's gay anyway?"

"Because they're gay," says Jeff, pitching a stick down the hill and watching as the dogs fall all over themselves trying to get to it. "They all know each other."

"Get out," Nick says again, laughing. "You guys aren't gay."

I look at Megan, who looks at Jeff. We're all thinking the same thing: Is it possible Nick really has no clue?

"You've met my girlfriend, Nick," says Megan. "You know, Lily."

"The chick with the long black hair?" Nick says. "I thought she was just your roommate."

"Yeah, well, you and Lily's mother," says Megan. "But

she really is my girlfriend. I have the scars on my thighs to prove it."

Jeff laughs as Nick's face falls. "And you're gay, too?" he asks me.

"I'm afraid so," I tell him.

"No way," Nick replies. "You're not gay. I'd know if you were gay."

"You want me to give you some hard proof?" I ask him, glancing meaningfully at his crotch.

Nick turns red. I can tell he's thinking about the couple of times he's given me rides home from the park in his truck and our legs have been pressed together while our dogs crawled from lap to lap.

"There are more gay people at the park than there are heteros," Jeff informs Nick. And he's right. Our part of town is a haven for lesbians, and slowly but surely the boys are discovering it as well. And all of us have dogs.

"Yeah?" Nick says. "Who else?"

I think for a second. "Brian," I say.

"Brian's gay?" Nick says, shocked.

"And Gretchen," adds Megan.

Nick gets a funny look on his face, but doesn't say anything.

"Oh, and Lori and Scott and Nancy," I rattle off quickly.

The look on Nick's face gets even stranger. "Oh, my God," he says.

"It's not that bad," says Megan. "It's not like we're forming a secret society or anything. We'll still let you come here."

"It's not that," Nick says. "It's just that..."

"What?" I say when he stops talking.

"Well, it's just that I sort of asked Gretchen out once. Nancy too."

"Get out," I say, adopting his favorite expression.

He nods his head. "Both in the same week. I wondered why they said no. I thought maybe they just didn't like me."

"You didn't know they were dykes?" Jeff says. "Geez, even I knew that. Gretchen pitches for the dyke softball team that plays here every Wednesday. She's got a mean arm."

"All those girls on that team are *dykes*?" Nicks says, as if this is the last straw.

"Come on," says Megan. "Even Lily's mother would be able to figure that one out. Those gals are the biggest bunch of daggers to ever hurl a ball. Oh, except for the catcher. I think we're supposed to call her Stephen now."

"I thought they were just, you know, sporty," Nick says, defeated. "I mean, my best friend in college was a girl on the softball team. She was the coolest. We used to watch football together, and she could put back more beer than I could. And she wasn't a…"

He stops talking when he sees us all staring at him.

"No way," he groans. "She was, wasn't she?"

"Did she have the requisite dyke softball haircut?" asks Megan.

"Long in back and short everywhere else," I say, helping Nick out.

He nods.

"Short fingernails?" Megan continues. "Drove an old Volvo?"

"It was her parents' old car," Nick says helplessly.

"But the TOWANDA! bumper sticker was all hers," Megan says confidently.

"I always wondered what that sticker meant," Nick says. "She told me it was the name of her old summer camp."

"I hate to break it to you, my friend, but you are officially a dyke hag," announces Megan.

"Enough about Nick's erotic fascination with beanos," Jeff says. "Let's get back to this Bruce Willis thing."

"You're fascinated by that," says Megan teasingly. "Would *you* sleep with Bruce Willis?"

"No," he says. "I'm not gay."

"But if you were gay," I ask him. "Would you sleep with him?"

"I don't think so," Jeff says. "He's too chunky. That's not my type."

"Oh, really?" I say, curious. "And just who would you want to sleep with?"

Jeff thinks about it for a minute. "I'd want to sleep with Tim Allen," he says finally.

"Tim Allen?" Megan and I say in unison.

"What?" says Jeff. "I just think he'd be good in bed, that's all. You know, he uses tools, so he would probably be good with his hands. And he looks OK in flannel. I like flannel."

"I know what you mean," Nick joins in. "He seems nice, kind of like your best friend from college or something."

"Not *your* best friend, apparently," Megan reminds him, and he turns red.

I'm too busy thinking about the possibility of Nick sleeping with some of his guy friends in college to say anything. Besides, I'm stunned by the whole Tim Allen revelation. The four of us stand there in silence, watching our dogs for a few more minutes until it's time to go. Then we leash them up and head our separate ways, Jeff to his car, Nick to his truck, and Megan and I down the street toward our houses.

"Can you believe those two?" says Megan when we stop to let the dogs pee. "Tim Allen."

I shudder. "Straight people are so weird," I say. "I just don't get them."

That's *Mr.*
Faggot to You

In 1996 a young man named Jamie Nabozny won a lawsuit against the Ashland school district in his home state of Wisconsin. What made the court victory so interesting was that Nabozny wasn't suing because he'd received an inadequate education or because an overbearing gym teacher forced him to do too many squat thrusts. He sued the school because as a student there he'd been physically and mentally abused for being queer and the administration did nothing to stop it.

The details of Nabozny's case are disturbing. Over a period of years, he was repeatedly taunted and roughed up. At the most extreme, he was urinated on, and, once, punched in the stomach so hard that he required hospitalization for internal bleeding. Much of this abuse went on with the knowledge of the school faculty, and despite repeated requests by Nabozny and his parents, the school refused to do anything about the harassment. When Nabozny's mother requested a transfer for her son, she was told that there was no school in Wisconsin where an openly gay boy would be safe and that Jamie should just get used to it.

At the trial the school administrators denied any knowledge of Nabozny or his troubles. Many said they didn't even know who he was. But testimony from former students told a much different story, and ultimately the Ashland school district was found negligent in protecting the civil rights of Jamie Nabozny. An out-of-court settlement was reached for a sum just under $1 million.

I find the Nabozny case interesting because I had a somewhat similar, although nowhere near as severe, experience in school. It started when I was about to enter the fifth grade and my father retired from his government job and moved us to the small town in upstate New York where he'd grown up. He had happy memories of the place, and he wanted me to grow up somewhere safe and pleasant, as he had.

But the reality was much different for me than it had been for him 40 years earlier. He'd been a hotshot athlete, captain of several teams and holder of many school records. I couldn't make a free throw if someone held me over the basket. He'd been very outgoing and had a lot of friends. I was introverted to the extreme. The idea of speaking to other human beings made me feel queasy, and anyway, I didn't see the point.

In short, I did not have a good time. Dropped into the middle of an insular farming town where everyone had grown up together, I did not blend. Within ten minutes of my first day there, I became the school queer. Granted, it originally had more to do with being an outsider than with any actual knowledge of my sexuality, but it was a label that stuck with me for the next seven years, until I refused to go back after the 11th grade.

To tell the truth, I hadn't thought a lot about life at Poland Central School until I read about the Nabozny case. Then, like a bad dream, it all came rushing back. Suddenly I recalled vividly what it felt like to one morning look at the class roster taped to my homeroom teacher's desk and see the word "faggot" written next to my name in red pen. She hadn't bothered to cross it out.

Or the day my best friend, the school's other misfit because of his bad haircut and weight problem, told me his mother (an alcoholic welfare cheat with a string of abusive boyfriends) didn't want him talking to me any more because she'd heard I might try to make him "that way."

Unlike Nabozny, I was never physically abused. No one ever hit me. No one pushed my head in the toilet. But it was just as bad for different reasons, mostly emotional. When Ray Donaldson grabbed his dick in the shower room after I'd spent a miserable 45 minutes trying to just not screw up in gym class and told me to get on my knees and suck him off, I never feared that he would actually make me do it. What I feared more was that I actually *wanted* to do it. Later, as I lay on my bed jerking off and obeying Ray's order in my mind, I came despite my hatred for him.

When I remember those years—day after day of dreading getting on the bus and week after week of waiting for 3 o'clock to come so it would be over—I know something of what Nabozny's life must have been like. So when I think of him depositing that million-dollar check, I smile to myself and hope he spends it on something he's always wanted. He certainly deserves it.

But there's another victory that Nabozny will have to wait a few more years to feel the effects of. See, no matter how much money he gets, it doesn't change the reasons he was picked on. It doesn't give him a chance to kick his tormentors where it counts. No amount of money in the world can make the kids who beat him up understand why they're the losers and make him see that he's come out on top after all. But time just might.

Eight years after I left high school, I received a phone call from someone I'd gone to high school with. A transfer student like I was, Charles Canterbury was a smart kid with a wicked sense of humor. He and I became friends, at least until he realized that he could finally gain some small amount of prestige with the rest of the school crowd by picking on me and another kid, John, who was also suspected of being queer.

I solved the problem by leaving school and going to college a year early. John remained and endured the torture of Charles and his friends, which included repeated calls to John's parents informing them that their son was a "cocksucker" and frequent burnings of gasoline on their front lawn.

Charles said he'd called me because he was thinking about how great things were back in high school and he wanted to see what I was up to because we'd been such good friends. Then he brought up John's name. "I called him the other day to say hello," Charles said. "He said I'd ruined his life back then and he had nothing to say to me. Then he hung up. Can you believe what an asshole he is?"

I made up some excuse to get off the phone and hung up myself. I was shaking, not from fear but from anger. Back in school I had wanted to kill Charles Canterbury for the way he'd treated me, John, and other people just to save himself. I'd even plotted various ways to do it. Now, eight years later, I couldn't even tell him we'd never really been friends at all. And to make things worse, he didn't even seem to remember any of it.

Periodically over the next two years I would think about that telephone call and be filled with rage. Then one day I opened my mail to find an invitation to my ten year reunion. Never mind that I'd never actually graduated or gotten a diploma, I was being invited back to see everyone who had made my life miserable a decade earlier.

The letter was filled with buoyant paragraphs about how high school had been "the best time of our lives" and how the reunion was a chance to catch up with "the friends who provided our fondest memories." At the bottom was a handwritten note from the reunion organizer, a girl who had said maybe two words (and not kind ones) to me during our entire seven years attending the same school. "Dear Mike," it said. "I really hope you come. We had such good times together!"

Attached to the invitation was a questionnaire asking us to write an update of our lives to be included in the reunion souvenir program. I wrote the following in the space provided:

Michael Thomas Ford is very proud to announce that he is still queer, despite the best attempts of his schoolmates to convince him that it is an unacceptable lifestyle. He would also like to take this opportunity to tell everyone he went to school with that he is happier, more successful, and a great deal more attractive than they are.

My entry did not appear in the program (I had my sister get one and check), but writing it made me let go of a lot of feelings I discovered I'd been carrying around. And looking through the pages of pictures of my balding, bloated classmates with their dreary lives and stained memories of a time when they'd once felt important, I realized that everything I'd written was indeed true. I hope one day Jamie Nabozny gets to do the same.

A Better Mousetrap

The Baptists are pissed off again. All 15 million of them. As if they didn't have enough to do—what with picketing Planned Parenthood offices, yanking copies of *Daddy's Roommate* from library shelves, and complaining about the immoral nature of American politics. Now it seems they're angry at Mickey Mouse. Or at least with his parent company.

It started with *Ellen*. Way back when Ellen finally told the world what some of us had known for a long time, the Baptists started squawking about how Disney, which produced the show, had no business feeding "gay propaganda" to millions of households every week. They also got all excited over Disney's policy of extending benefits to the domestic partners—gay or straight—of their employees.

This was all too much for the delicate sensibilities of the Bible-waving set, and they complained loudly that Disney's actions were decidedly "antifamily" and "pro-homosexual." They'd had enough, they said, and they were determined to put an end to it once and for all. After giving the folks at Disney fair warning, they announced that they were going to bring the Mouse to his knees by boycotting anything that had even a passing relationship to Disney. They predicted that within weeks Disney would renounce the demon of homosexuality and come crawling back, begging for forgiveness and lost dollars.

Well, that certainly was a lot of enraged polyester and hair spray for the folks at the House that Mickey Built to face. And the Baptists did have one small tactical advantage working for them. It was almost summer, and Disney was about to release its latest assault on American consumers. *Hercules* was due in theaters in a matter of weeks, and Disney was counting on the film to bring in huge bucks. It had created a dizzying array of merchandise, and all across this great land of ours stores were stocking up on lunch boxes, backpacks, hand puppets, posters, key rings, inflatable pool toys, and anything else *Hercules*-related. The Baptists knew this, of course, and they crowed that their shunning of the Wonderful World of Disney was going to cost the company millions of dollars.

And they were right. After all, children are Disney's target audience, and the Baptists have a good many of them under their control. They are not entirely stupid people, and they had done the math. Assuming that each of the 15 million families dedicated to the boycott had two kids and two happily married, nondivorced parents, that added up to a total of 60 million people who would not be seeing *Hercules*. With an average national ticket price of about $6, that meant a revenue loss of $360 million for Disney.

That didn't even begin to include the losses the company would have to take when those 30 million Baptist children took the money earmarked for Hercules skateboards, video games, and hairbrushes and spent it instead on wholesome playthings that instilled a sense of self-righteousness and piety. After tallying up these impressive figures, the Baptists were sure they had the game in the bag.

But there's something they forgot to factor into the equation—the enemy against which they were waging their holy war. See, after children, Disney's biggest audience is queens. Gay men are simply mad about Disney, and there are even more of us than there are Baptist children. And we have a lot more cash.

So now back to the math. First we had the 50 million queens who were sure to be beating down the doors to the theaters on opening day. That was a good $300 million right there (more, actually, since ticket prices in New York had just jumped to $9 and there is no such thing as a matinee price in the city). And since most of them would see the movie at least twice, you could just go ahead and double that to $600 million or so right off the bat.

And let us not forget the albums, dolls, T-shirts, animation cels, and ceramic figurines all of those boys would be picking up for their collections. The children's toy market is lucrative; the adult collector market is even more so. A Baptist child with a $20 bill and a craving for a single Hercules action figure is no match for a Disney queen with a platinum Visa card and a loft filled with framed limited edition lithographs. I'm not so good with accounting, but even I could see that queers would be pumping several billion dollars into Disney's pockets by July 4 weekend.

There was one more thing the Baptists hadn't thought through before making their proclamation of victory. Did they really expect us to believe that they could make it through the summer listening to all 30 million of their God-fearing children whine incessantly about being the *only* ones at school who hadn't seen *Hercules* while their parents popped another *David and Jonathan: Bible Best Friends* video into the VCR? Did they really think they had the willpower to refuse buying all of those Hercules pajamas, Hercules posters, and Hercules board games? And how-oh-how did they ever imagine they could survive the long hot days of summer without once stopping into McDonald's for those Happy Meals with *Hercules* prizes? Maybe they thought they could just pray through it all. I wished them luck, but I suspected that somewhere around July 15 they would give up and start sneaking, cleverly disguised as lapsed Catholics, to their local multiplexes.

And they did. The Baptist boycott was a total bust. Sure, Disney probably lost a couple of million here and there, but what's that to them? The amount queers spent on their products never wavered and in fact probably increased a little bit because, after all, what gay man can resist a muscle-bound Greek god in a toga? Beaten back, the Baptists went home and licked their wounds.

They remained quiet for a while, too. But now they've decided to go after the Mouse again. Apparently they're all excited because of a minor victory in which they convinced American Airlines to issue an announcement that it would no longer be offering any "special privileges" to its gay employees or gay customers and that it would stop actively recruiting a queer consumer base by advertising in gay periodicals. I don't know any gay person who would want to fly American anyway, given its lousy service and horrendous food, but that's another story. But this success has apparently emboldened the Baptists, and now they're back.

This time the Baptists are steamed that the Disney theme parks hold annual Gay Days, where throngs of queers take over the parks for a weekend of frolicking during Gay Pride Month. While these are not official Disney-sponsored events (anyone can rent the park for a day), the Baptists insist that having them at all is an assault on traditional family values. Well, on *their* traditional family values anyway. Instead of just staying away, they once more announced that they will have a financial boycott of the parks.

Knowing that this financial blackmail backfired on them the last time they tried it, the Right decided to go one step further. Recently, in an apparent attempt to up the pressure, the Rev. Pat Robertson warned the city of Orlando, Fla., where Disney World is located, that its continued support of the gay community would bring dire consequences. "I would warn Orlando that you're right in the way of some serious hurricanes, and I don't think I'd be waving those flags in God's face if I were you," he said in a TV broadcast. The flags in question were gay pride banners the city was flying throughout the month of June. And it wasn't just hurricanes the reverend was concerned with. He also predicted that tolerance of queer folks "will bring terrorist bombings. It will bring earthquakes, tornadoes, and possibly a meteor." This, of course, is in addition to the 15 million enraged Baptists.

But despite the threat of becoming the modern-day Sodom and Gomorrah, the city of Orlando did not cancel gay pride observances. Nor did any disaster—natural or otherwise—ruin the queer takeover of Disney World, which went off without a hitch. All I can figure is that once God got a look at the production numbers in the *Beauty and the Beast* live show, he was having such a good time that he forgot all about his original reason for coming.

Whatever the reasons for the sparing of Disney World, I have news for the good Baptists and those like them: This isn't about being pro-anything except pro-money. Call it a battle between good and evil or between damnation and salvation. Call it a cultural Armageddon, with Jesus taking on Mickey. The fact is, it's all about profits.

As much as I'm proud of Disney for not caving in to these moral rednecks, I know enough to not be too impressed. After all, those annual Gay Days bring Disney piles of cash. You can't take over a park without paying for the privilege. And *Ellen* was only on the air as long as it kept pulling in sponsor dollars. Once it started to sag in the ratings and advertisers fled the sinking ship, it pulled the plug and never looked back, even to say thank you.

As for the partner benefits, I'd like to see any part of the Disney corporation run for even a day once all of the lesbian and gay designers, animators, writers, ticket takers, actors, pretzel vendors, dancers, accountants, and walk-around characters go on strike if those benefits are taken away. Then the right-wingers would have their gay-free parks, but how would they explain to their grandkids that Chip and Dale weren't there to greet them because after hours they were doing things that were against nature, or that they couldn't ride Splash Mountain after all because the operator was a rug-muncher who resigned because she thought Jesus was an asshole?

No, if the religious zealots really want to make an impact on Disney, they're going to have to do better than this. They're going to have to shell out big bucks to hold their own "Crazy Christers Days" at Disneyland. They're going to have to make their own movies to compete with Disney's. They're going to have to get a lot more talented so they can take over all of the jobs vacated by the queers who won't work for Disney any more.

In short, they're going to have to get a whole lot smarter. Because this isn't about who's right and who's wrong. It's not about this ridiculous "pro-family/antifamily" nonsense. Disney doesn't give a damn about principles, either conservative or liberal. No American, profit-driven corporation gives a damn about principles. Corporations care about who's paying for their annual bonuses. And the bad news for the religious right folks is that there are a whole lot more of us than there are of them.

Do You Hear What I Hear?

I just found out I have lesbian ears. You don't know how happy I am about it. When I heard all the news reports a couple of weeks ago announcing that scientists had discovered a difference between the inner ears of lesbians and those of straight women, suddenly my entire life fell into place.

Yes, I know I'm a man. It doesn't matter. My ears are definitely dykes. Finally, I have an excuse for why I prefer the Indigo Girls over the Pet Shop Boys, and why I can remember the lyrics to all of Melissa Etheridge's songs but run screaming from the room whenever anyone plays a Barbra Streisand tune.

It's my lesbian ears. Like those of a Labrador, they are apparently tuned in only to certain frequencies. Those that are pleasant and agreeable—such as the smoky tones of k. d. lang—are received with joy and ushered straight into the brain. Others are the vocal equivalent of a high-frequency warning whistle that only dogs can hear. When confronted with them, my lesbian ears go into emergency mode and shut down entirely, preventing me from being exposed to anything that might cause irreparable harm, like Mariah Carey and Celine Dion singles.

This is exciting. I've always said that I make a better lesbian than I do a gay man. Now I know why. It's my inner ears. All these years I thought I just wasn't doing it right or that maybe my social conditioning had leaned too heavily toward encouraging a fondness for hummus and an appreciation of softball. But now I know it's all because I've been hearing things differently my entire life. Thank heavens for science.

And I think I can predict with a reasonable amount of certainty that this ear thing is only the beginning. Surely it's only a matter of time before these same intrepid scientists conduct further studies and stumble across the miraculous Flannel Gene, responsible for an otherwise unaccountable desire to purchase vast quantities of L.L. Bean products. Right behind that would come the discovery of the oh-so-important Gertrude Stein Extender, a heretofore unknown muscle found in the tongue that renders those who possess it capable of amazing feats of oral sex.

Then again, maybe nothing more will come of this. Remember when they decided that the brains of gay men are different from those of straight men? That was a big deal for a while. Everyone was all excited about it. Then—poof—it just disappeared. We haven't heard anything about it for weeks.

I can't say why this happened, exactly, but I have a suspicion that once the scientists did more tests, they discovered that not only were the brains of gay men different from those of their straight brothers, they were also superior. I wouldn't be at all shocked to learn that the area of the frontal lobe they found so fascinating turned out to hold the secrets to a highly developed sense of aesthetics, a fine-tuned wit, and the ability to dance. In straight men, on the other hand, the very same area had evolved into a repository for useless team sports statistics, endless data regarding the proper use of snow tires, and arcane barbecuing skills. Not wanting to let this knowledge fall into the wrong hands, further investigations were shut down immediately and all findings turned over to the CIA.

The same thing could happen with this lesbian ear business. Think about what a threat it is to the safety of society. After all, if they can figure out what makes dyke ears so unique, how long will it be before some enterprising plastic surgeon develops a procedure for reshaping the ears of straight women to match those of their muff-munching counterparts? All over the world, women sick of enduring the straight men in their lives will be lining up for the procedure that will rescue them from heterosexual hell and transform them into sisters who embark on thrilling new lives accompanied by Cris Williamson warbling, "Filling up and spilling over like an endless waterfall..." Once the additional Sapphic Fingers procedure is performed, they will also be able to do the accompanying hand motions flawlessly.

It's the religious right's worst nightmare—queerness on demand. Of course, as with everything else right-wingers don't agree with, at first they would try to get people to see lesbian ears as undesirable, even unhealthy. Claiming all kinds of unprovable side effects and dangers, they would warn the curious away by waving red flags of their own pernicious design. In a last ditch effort at halting public interest, they would inevitably try to turn lesbian ears into a birth defect, much as they've done with homosexuality in general. "Love the listener, not the ears!" would be their rallying cry as they circle the re-alignment boutiques.

But ultimately their efforts would be futile. Thanks to lesbian chic, women worldwide would soon be rushing to the nearest clinic for the latest in cosmetic surgery. It would be the newest cool thing to do. You enter on Friday a bland, middle-class housewife sick of making tuna noodle casserole and pretending that giving your husband head is your wildest dream, and exit on Monday a freewheeling, Subaru-driving lesbian with an all-access pass to the Michigan Womyn's Music Festival and a sack full of sex toys. The Crazy Christers' only consolation: At least it will give them something else to blow up when they're not busy at the abortion clinics.

Straight men, of course, would not be so quick to jump on the bandwagon. After all, brain surgery is slightly more complicated than merely realigning the inner ear. But once somebody very high-profile made being gay a mark of the new masculinity, then everyone would be doing it. After all, look what football players wearing earrings did for that particular fad in the early '80s. And it's a well-known fact that after Dennis Rodman made cross-dressing the latest in macho pastimes, sales of size 12 women's footwear and extra-large Victoria's Secret ensembles went through the roof.

All it would take to make the gay brain transplant procedure a hit with men everywhere is a good spokesman. I suggest Bruce Willis. After all, he's already married to the perfect lesbian equivalent. The only thing Demi Moore is lacking to make her a full-fledged dyke icon is that inner ear thing, and I'm sure she'd do it if the price were right. She did *Striptease* for only $2 million, and I know we could raise that much with a countrywide lesbian wheat-free bake sale. Once she signs on, Bruce is sure to follow, and if the two of them both undergo the change, they can send their careers into the stratosphere by becoming the most celebrated gay Hollywood couple since Ellen and Anne.

If John Travolta and Kirstie Alley can make the muddleheaded edicts of Scientology appealing to the masses, surely Bruce and Demi can make something as inherently fabulous as being queer the Next Big Thing. They'd just need a catchy slogan—perhaps something like Make the Switch—accompanied by pictures of smiling men and women frolicking somewhere sunny while holding fruit drinks and enjoying their new brains and inner ears.

With enough celebrity endorsement, turning gay would become the trend of the millennium. And why not? After all, the world is entering a new age. It's completely natural for people to want to embrace change and head boldly into the next century. Just like piercings and tattoos, inner ear and brain modification would sweep the nation, and before long even suburban teenagers would be rushing to their local shops and lining up for the procedures.

Imagine if you will a group of teenage girls at the mall one afternoon. They're hanging out at the Gap. Weary of trying on yet even more pairs of khakis and really cute shirts and having already seen the latest Leonardo DiCaprio movie 16 times, they decide to do something different.

"Come on," Tiffany says to her girlfriends. "Let's head over to Switchers and watch Amber go gay!"

"I don't know," says Amber, who has been thinking about doing this for a while but is still a bit unsure. "My mom would kill me. You know how much she's been looking forward to the prom and all. She wanted me to wait until after that. I have my dress and everything. Besides, what would I tell Jason?"

"Are you going to not do something just because a *boy* doesn't want you to?" asks Tiffany. "That is so '80s."

After another few minutes of indecision, Amber decides that she really does want to have her ears done. Besides, they're giving away the new Ani DiFranco with every pair of ears, and how can she pass that up?

Once in the salon, they all stand around the table as Amber prepares for the big moment. Perhaps one of her more daring friends even holds her hand as the technician inserts the special ear realignment device.

"Take a deep breath," she says, and before Amber can even exhale, it's all over.

"Wow," she says, beaming up at her friends with an entirely new perspective on things. "That didn't hurt at all. And hey, have I told you that you all look really cute today?"

The technician, after explaining to Amber how she shouldn't use her new ears too much for about two weeks, sends her on her way with a photocopied sheet of aftercare instructions and a copy of *Now That You Know* for her parents.

The results of the gay brain procedure would be even more dramatic. Imagine showing up at work one day to discover that your office mate, Phil, has suddenly removed all of the Chicago Bulls posters from his walls and replaced them with framed Japanese-inspired posters of cats from the Metropolitan Museum of Art.

"Hey Ed," Phil says cheerfully, a fresh lilt in his voice. "How was your weekend?"

"Great," you say. "I saw some friends. How about yourself?"

"Oh, you know," Phil responds. "A little of this, a little of that. Say, when is gay pride this year? You're going to go, right?"

For a moment you're taken aback. Phil has never asked you about your life before, or rather about your *gay* life. In fact, he's usually the one to be standing at the water cooler telling anyone who will listen about all the women he's scored with since Friday afternoon.

"Um, it's in a couple of weeks," you answer, noticing for the first time that his normally bad haircut has been replaced by a short, sleek new look. Why, is that a glint of gel you see lifting the front into a razor-straight line?

"Great," says Phil, brushing a stray bit of thread from the sleeve of his suit coat, a beautiful Armani three-button number you've never seen him wear before. "Maybe we can all get together for brunch that weekend."

Suddenly you realize what's happened. Phil has undergone the change.

"Hey," you say happily. "Did someone get a new brain this weekend?"

Phil grins. "Well, I didn't want to say anything," he says. "It seemed tacky to point it out, like asking if you like my new haircut or something. By the way, you do like it, don't you?"

After that it's cappuccinos all around.

But these scenarios will be a long time coming. In the meantime, those of us who already have lesbian ears need to do something about it. While having such rare and beautiful things is special indeed, it also means that we're missing out on a few parts of everyday life. For example, I suggest campaigning for specialized products, like Gay Boy earphones that direct sound through our uniquely constructed passages, allowing us to listen to all of that music we've been hearing incorrectly for years. I, for one, would like to understand once and for all the fuss being made over Madonna.

Or maybe we could get specially designed Queer Ear Q-Tips, constructed with a unique bent allowing them to swab the most hidden recesses free of waxy buildup. Then there would be specialized eardrops, earplugs, and anything else one could stick inside these wondrously designed canals of ours. If we're going to be unusual, we should at least have our own merchandise. After all, isn't that the whole point of being different?

No More Mr. Nice Guy

I'm happy for Ellen. I really am. I wish her all the luck in the world now that she's come out. I hope she shows millions of people that gays and lesbians can be just like everyone...

Oh, who am I kidding? I just can't do it any more. I can't keep pretending that this is the best thing that's happened to queers since Stonewall. I don't want to have an *Ellen* party. I don't want to get yet another mass E-mail trumpeting the joys of finally seeing ourselves regularly on national television. I don't want any of it.

The truth is, I don't care if straight people like the new and improved Ellen. I don't care if they like any of us. In fact, sometimes I wish the whole lot of them would just bite me.

Do I sound crabby? Maybe I am. But the fact of the matter is, I'm tired of being nice. I'm tired of worrying about what sort of image I give straight people of the gay community. I'm tired of trying to make them like us.

It isn't just this Ellen thing, either. It's the gay marriage thing and the adoption thing and the being on the school board thing. I'm the first one to agree that we deserve all the rights that everyone else has. But I'm tired of trying to fit in to get them. Everywhere I look, we're bending over backward to be nice so that straight people will like us or at least pretend to. We're trying to show them that we can be as harmless and inoffensive and, yes, normal as they are.

Well, I don't want to be normal. Or harmless.

There's a scene in the wonderful movie *Stonewall* where some dykes and fags are preparing to go talk to straight folks about what it's like to be queer. The woman instructing the group lays out a very strict dress code: Skirts and blouses for the women, shirts and ties (but no stripes or plaids) for the men. That scene filled me with rage, not because of how the queers were downplaying their actual selves, but because they *had* to do it to get their point across.

Later in the film the police make their now-infamous raid on the Stonewall Inn. As one of the main characters, a drag queen, is being led away, the cop manhandling her says, "I bet you don't know whether you want to kiss me or hit me." When the queen makes her choice and decks him, setting off the cinematic version of the riots, I felt the anger that had been building up inside me flood out in a joyous torrent of pride.

Then I pick up a magazine and read yet another article about this whole *Ellen* thing, and I realize that we're still staring that cop in the face, trying to make up our minds. Only now we're afraid to hit him, because it might make us look bad. Instead, we try to figure out the best way to be so bland, so ordinary, so mainstream that he can't help but like us because, well, golly, we're just like him. And as long as we don't try to make a pass at him or anything, he thinks he might just leave us alone after all.

Almost 30 years after Stonewall, we're still afraid to wear stripes and plaids.

I once had neighbors, teenage boys who didn't like queers, despite the fact that almost every single house on the street had some of us in residence. These kids had terrorized the neighborhood for years. Their constant harassment drove out the diesel dyke and her gay room-mate who lived next door. Cars with rainbow stickers routinely had windows smashed. When I moved in, they thought I was OK. Until I put up a rainbow flag. Then it disappeared, and they started bragging about having stolen it.

I thought about being diplomatic—talking to them, maybe to their parents, telling them what they did wasn't cool and that we all had to live together and respect one another. But then I got angry, at them for thinking they could get away with their behavior, but more at myself for letting them make me afraid to confront them head-on and tell them what I really felt about them.

I bought ten rainbow flags and gave them to all the neighbors. We all hung them up. The next time I saw the boys outside, playing basketball with their friends, I went out on my porch. "See all these flags," I said, point-ing to the rows of fluttering rainbows. "This means there are more of us than there are of you. Don't you ever for-get that." I got my flag back, and we never had another problem with those boys.

I was reminded of that incident recently when I ran into some similar trouble, only in a very different envi-ronment. It happened not on my street but on the infor-mation superhighway.

One of the truly great horrors of computer technology is that people who should never be allowed to open their mouths now have an opportunity to share their opinions with others. Don't get me wrong; I'm all for free speech. After all, I wouldn't have a job without it. And I do think the sharing of ideas is just about the only thing that keeps America from turning into one great big Barbie play set.

But there are limits to my patience.

To find proof of freedom of expression gone awry, you have only to look at the user profiles that members of online services create to describe themselves to the world. Take, for instance, America Online. This happens to be the service I use, only because I'm far too lazy to find another one. One of the few fun things about AOL is that you can search the member directory using key phrases that other users might have included in their profiles.

For example, say you're into llamas. You can type the word "llama" into the search engine and moments later be rewarded with a list of AOL users who have that word somewhere in their profiles (there are 83, in case you were wondering). Now, the search isn't entirely discriminating, and you could end up with people who list llamas as an interest as well as people who say they like men who look like llamas. Still, you get the idea.

A few months ago, hot, bored, and avoiding a deadline, I was playing around online. After finding out how many AOLers were both hairy and into boxer shorts (a staggering 289) and locating my former college roommate online (he lists his hobbies as evangelical Christianity, DC Comics, and the Bible), I decided to try something new using the member search. I typed the words "gay bashing" into the search engine. What came back was a list of 16 AOL members who had those words in their profiles. Intrigued, I looked at each one in turn.

Of the 16, nine turned out to be fellow queers who wrote things like "bashing gay bashers back" under their hobbies or who for whatever reason had the combination of "gay" and "basher" in their profiles, even if they weren't connected.

The other seven were more interesting, as they were from members who listed gay bashing as an actual hobby. But that wasn't the best part. The real fun was reading their grammatically incorrect, inherently moronic attempts at getting their messages, such as they were, across. See, stupid people as a group (think Congress or the antiabortion movement) at least generally have carefully thought-out group statements to hide behind. But when individuals are left to spontaneously speak for themselves (think Newt Gingrich or Ralph Reed), then the real idiocy of their ideas is revealed.

Here, then, are my favorites, complete with all of their original spellings and jolly wit.

Basher0001: Judging from his screen name, the founder of the bashing movement. Written in all caps, his message was simple, to the point, and slightly confused about the use of plural nouns: "Bashing gay, bi, lesbian and all the other crap out there!!!" I think he missed a spot.

Aidsinacan: I suppose this fellow gets points for the screen name, although I suspect the guy who invented cheese in a can is probably more likely to be remembered fondly. This keeper lists his name as "Stain" and puts as his favorite pastimes "gay bashing, black bashing, smoking weed!" His optional member quote: "F@%$ all blacks." At least he's inclusive in his stupidity.

KingGump: I'm not exactly sure what being the King of Gump entails, but I'd hate to be part of the royal family, especially considering the delightful party games played by his majesty: "Making fun of homos like my brother and Eltin John." Gee, I guess George Michael will have to play at the inaugural ball alone. Or maybe that's Jorge Michael.

Penzilz: Listed under the clever member names Joe and Jane Baptist, these obviously dull pencil heads give their professions as "attorneys for HMOs." Utilizing one of the most irritating of all grammatical errors, they state, "If God meant men to be with men he'd of made it genetic." Perhaps they learned to write so well from reading the redneck version of the Bible.

SupertoneX: Truly a rebel, this daring AOL member bills himself as John O'Cloud, IRA Member. His hobbies, when not terrorizing British troops, presumably, are "gay bashing, golf, and girls who aren't ugly." Like the Penzilz before him, he also claims knowledge of the Almighty's inner workings, stating, "God created alcohol so the Irish wouldn't rule the world." Apparently it worked.

This was quite a group to work with. At first, I thought about simply reporting them all to the powers that be. AOL is nothing if not a bureaucratic entity. It has rules for everything, including what you can name yourself and what you can tell others about yourself. One of the no-nos is putting racist, sexist, or otherwise discriminatory statements in your member profile. Numerous times, folks posting on the gay and lesbian message boards, myself included, have had their messages pulled for being "offensive" in some obscure way. It's called getting TOSsed, or being punished for violating the Terms of Service.

Again, I'm the most anticensorship fellow around. But I do have a mean streak, and it's fun to make stupid people suffer. Having to rename themselves or change their profiles is exactly what would piss off these online bigots the most. So, feeling like the world's biggest tattletale, I did report some of them. But not all of them. I saved the best ones for myself.

I started by subscribing all of them to every electronic gay news service I could think of. This is the E-mail version of sending in the "bill me later" subscription cards from magazines to people you don't like. Within days their mailboxes are filled with post after post enlightening them about the issues facing the queer community. They don't have to read them, but just seeing them there is probably enough to make them uncomfortable. Besides, while getting onto those lists is as easy as entering an E-mail address, getting off again is next to impossible. Once your name is circulated and copied thousands of times in a single day, you're soon receiving every gay-related thing out there.

The next thing I did was establish a new screen name—SuperFag. My personal profile listed my hobbies as "hunting down homophobes and hanging their heads in my den." I then set up a buddy list for this account with the names of all my gay-bashing friends on it. This handy AOL function allows you to see whenever someone is signed on at the same time you are. You can also see what area of the service the person is accessing.

Periodically I would sign on under my new name and see who was around. Inevitably, at least one of the bashing brigade would be there. When I found him or her, I would immediately send an E-mail with the simple message "We're watching you." If the user happened to be in a chat room, I would go there and inform the entire room that a homophobe was present. Generally the other occupants of the room would start harassing the basher and continue until she or he left.

I had already set the preferences on my vigilante account so that I could not receive E-mail from anyone. If any of my prey did try to reply to my E-mails or respond to my terrorism, they would be met with a "This member is not receiving mail from you" message, frustrating them even more. I was a stealth bomber, swooping through the AOL skies and strafing the backsides of whatever bigot got in my way.

One by one, the names on my list disappeared from AOL. Some of them returned in other guises, but I did regular searches of the member directory and updated my most-wanted roster. Usually it only took a couple of "We're watching you" E-mails before someone went into hiding. Why none of them ever thought to report *me* to AOL is a mystery. I suspect it's because they didn't want to admit to being badgered out of existence by a fag with a modem and too much free time.

Ultimately I got bored with confronting homophobes

online and deleted my screen name. But it was fun while it lasted, and it gave me a sense of accomplishment, much as standing up to the neighborhood bullies had. Of course, it's easy to be brave when all you're fighting is words on a screen. Actual physical confrontations are another thing altogether. Still, there's something rewarding about seeing someone run from you when you yell back, even if it is only electronically.

Sure, I tuned in to watch the now-infamous episode of *Ellen* and see television history being made. I think Ellen DeGeneres is a swell chick and very, very funny. And that guy who plays her cousin is just my type. But as for Ellen's television counterpart, I couldn't help but wish she'd stop worrying about offending people and just tell everyone to fuck off. It works for me.

Part Three

It's All About Me

Fitting In

I have a confession to make: I'm a bad fag. Seriously. Someone should take away my membership card immediately, because apparently I just don't belong on the team at all. I can't even be the water boy or the rainbow-suited mascot.

I've tried to fit in. I really have. Back when I first came out, I moved immediately to Greenwich Village because it was where gay men were supposed to live. I cut my hair really short, pierced my ear, and attended ACT UP meetings a few times. I went to bars, wore leather motorcycle boots, and even slept with a couple of people, including a UPS delivery guy, which at the time was a mark of true success.

OK, so I never did drag, took ecstasy, or went to the Saint Black Party and got fisted in a urinal. I didn't go to bars that often, never even thought about joining the Gay Men's Chorus, and wasn't up on the latest trendy restaurants. I was too busy worrying about how to really be gay to do all that stuff. Still, I did my best.

But it wasn't enough. The longer I stayed in New York, the more I realized I wasn't really cutting it as a queen. I didn't enjoy going out on weekends, let alone during the week; most nights I fell asleep with a book on my chest before my more vigorous gay brothers had even left their apartments. I couldn't care less about what Madonna was up to and didn't even own a cock ring.

Worst of all, I found myself completely unable to recognize when I was being cruised. Eventually I had to admit that I just wasn't doing it right.

At first this upset me. Why couldn't I fit in with the other gay boys? They all seemingly took to it so easily, as though they'd been born knowing exactly what kind of wine to serve with fish and with a natural inclination to enjoy art openings and benefit performances. Every last one of them seemed perfectly at home in a gym, and their hair always looked freshly cut. But no matter how hard I tried, my carefully rolled-up T-shirt sleeves always slumped by evening's end, I couldn't understand a single painting at MOMA, and no amount of gel would tame the cowlicks that made it impossible for me to have really cool hair. To make everything worse, I didn't see the charm in hanging out all night waiting for the right guy to notice me when I could be at home watching animal documentaries on the Discovery Channel.

Then, just as I was about to give up on ever being fabulous enough, something unexpected happened. Rising up defiantly from the liberal seas, a wave of conservatism swept over our gay land. Almost overnight, the reign of ACT UP was over, and suddenly we weren't supposed to be queer any more. Now we were supposed to be, in the hypnotic words of the leaders of this new movement, "just like everybody else."

Politically, this disturbed me. I had a vague notion that to be just like everybody else was to no longer exist. But secretly I was glad I could stop wearing my earring. The hole had gotten infected a few too many times, and I was sick of it. So I tossed it out, along with the motorcycle boots and the Queer Nation T-shirt.

I still got to keep my hair short, but now I was free to dress as badly as the straight guys at the office. Now that we (gay people) were just like everybody else, my horrible lack of fashion sense was no longer a disability. In fact, it made my transition into the world of "everybody else" much easier.

So there I was, being just like everyone else. It felt good. I talked about how important it was for "us" to have the same rights that "they" had so that we could indeed be just like them in nearly every way. I decided that gay marriage was a good thing and even dated one of its principal and most vocal proponents. Over dinner we talked about how wonderful it would be if we could have the same benefits our legally married straight friends had.

But again, after a couple months of this, something didn't feel quite right. Sure, it was nice to not have to worry about being different, and registering as a domestic partner at City Hall seemed very pioneering. But the truth was, being just like everybody else was, well, sort of boring. More than sort of. I looked around at my straight married friends, pictured years of holidays with in-laws and squabbling over what school the kids should go to, and felt a little queasy.

Deciding that being just like everybody else wasn't for me, I ditched the gay-marriage activist and became as gay as possible. But instead of aspiring to the carefree gay life I'd first tried, I focused on being meaningfully gay. Protecting the existence of the unique homo species became a mission. I came out to everyone I could think of, just so they would be aware that someone they knew was queer, a word I began using again now that I wasn't trying to be respectable. I wore gay buttons on my jacket and made sure I took the Monday after every gay pride weekend off so that everyone would see just how hard I'd been out being gay.

In my quest to be the ambassador of all that was gay, I went so far as to appear on the now-defunct *Jane Pratt Show,* talking about how bisexuals and their demand for equal attention were taking precious energy out of the real gay community. The audience applauded my logic, and Jane told me afterward how much more coherent I'd been than the other guests. Even though the producer told us not to mention the fact that at least one of Jane's former boyfriends, rocker Michael Stipe, was admittedly bisexual, it was all very thrilling.

Too thrilling. As it turned out, being so ardently gay was really exhausting. It meant paying close attention to the news and knowing absolutely everything about every item even remotely related to gay causes. It meant being ready to lecture my straight friends at the drop of a hat about how their support was necessary to achieve our goals. It meant not just using but actually understanding phrases such as "diversity-focused organizational schism" and "intracommunity issue assessment and goal enhancement infrastructure."

But the biggest problem was that it involved being angry. Really angry. All the time. About everything. Each day I would sit down with the paper and scan it for gay-related items. I would dutifully clip them out and read them. Then I would decide how angry to be about each one.

There was a decided hierarchy to gay issues, and the store of anger was meted out appropriately. Anything involving AIDS—in particular the government's slowness in fighting it and/or discrimination against people with it—was given top priority. This was the late '80s. Larry Kramer was everywhere, and we were all busy marching and screaming and generally misbehaving about the Crisis. It was good to be angry, fun even, and there was a lot to be angry about.

After AIDS came gays in the military, followed by adoption rights, the marriage thing, and general gay bashing. I duly noted each incident and thought long and hard about What Should Be Done About It. I kept bulging file folders filled with gay-related news stories. I was very informed, very angry, and, I thought, very, very gay.

The issue I ended up being the angriest about was the depiction of gays and lesbians in popular media. This was the fault of the Gay and Lesbian Alliance Against Defamation. I attended a meeting of the group with a friend. The topic that fateful night happened to be Rush Limbaugh, the virulently homophobic talk show host who was just coming to power in New York. GLAAD was trying to get Rush fired from his job because he "made us look bad."

After discussing Rush for a while, the conversation turned to how queers were being depicted in movies, in particular the just-released *The Silence of the Lambs*. It was the position of GLAAD that the movie perpetuated a stereotype of gays as psychopathic drag queens who minced around in too much blue eye shadow while talking to poodles. They wanted someone to write a letter about it to that bastion of uppity letter writing, *The Village Voice*. Overcome by my fervor to protect the gay family, I volunteered. Now, I'd seen *The Silence of the Lambs,* and it had never once occurred to me to be offended by the character everyone was getting upset about. But, caught up in the moment, I decided that maybe everyone was right and that this was my chance to do something about it. I wrote a most forceful letter, which appeared the next week in the *Voice* and got a lot of attention from my activist friends. But as I sat in my apartment and read it over and over again, all I could think about was how Jodie Foster would see it and never be my best friend.

I did a few more things with GLAAD, writing letters of protest about Sharon Stone's beaver shot in *Basic Instinct* and about the fact that Doug Savant's gay character on *Melrose Place* never got to kiss anyone. They appeared here and there, always to hearty approval from the people who read them. But my heart wasn't in it. When the group decided to protest *Sesame Street* because there had never been an openly gay Muppet, I decided it was time to move on.

The trouble was, there was nowhere else to go. I'd done the fabulous thing. I'd done the just-like-every-one-else thing. I'd done the activist thing. The only other thing left was the 12-step thing, which was suddenly hugely popular with a lot of queers. But never having done drugs or overindulged in alcohol (OK, not since my teens), it seemed unlikely that I would find my true calling there. And I'd been so busy trying to fit in that I hadn't had time for enough sex to qualify for Sexaholics Anonymous. I wasn't even a success at being unhealthily gay.

For a while I went into a depression, saddened by the fact that I just wasn't the queer I should be. Everywhere I looked, people were achieving greatness as the perfect examples of whatever banner they'd chosen to carry, whether it was being the reigning king of the party circuit or the activist with the most arrests under his belt. But there I was, stuck in the middle, neither one thing nor another.

Then, just as I began to think my only remaining option was to become straight, I woke up one morning with a revelation—I didn't have to be anything. I don't know why I'd never thought of it before. Probably because I was too busy being something I wasn't. But suddenly I started looking at the people around me in a new way, watching them as they scurried off to their meetings and parties, their protests and safer-sex orgies. They were so busy being gay that they weren't even living. Being gay was a career choice for them, not a way of life.

That was a decade ago. Since then I've figured out how to integrate being gay with being me. Yes, I still get angry about things. Yes, I think fighting for causes is important. But so are a lot of other things, things that have nothing to do with being gay. Like enjoying friends because they add something to my life, not because they have Really Deep Thoughts about the existence of a gay gene. Or laughing at Ellen because she's funny, not because she advanced the gay presence on network television. I might not always know which lawmakers are pro-gay and which ones aren't, but I understand when to get worked up and when to sit back with a pint of Ben & Jerry's World's Best Vanilla and watch the world go by like one big circus parade.

I may still be a bad fag, but now I'm a happy one. And Jodie, if you're reading this, I really loved you in *The Silence of the Lambs*. Will you ever forgive me?

Why Not Me?

"You're listening to what?" Katherine asks incredulously.

"Wynonna Judd," I mumble, quickly turning the volume down on the stereo so she can't hear any more through the phone.

"Why would you do that?"

"Um, I'm writing a review for someone," I lie, fumbling for a believable answer.

The truth is, I'm too embarrassed to tell her the real reason I'm listening to the album. Katherine and I have been friends for so long that she knows just about everything there is to know about me. Yet I just can't bring myself to admit to her that deep down in my heart, I want to be Wynonna.

Yes, it's true. I want to have big jouncing breasts and masses of thick red hair. I want full, pouty lips that curl up in an Elvis sneer. I want to caress my guitar while thousands of lesbians squeal in delight and wet their cheap vinyl seats as they watch me totter across the stage in tight cowboy boots. I can't help it.

I know there are classier people to want to be. Like k.d., for instance, or perhaps even Melissa. I'll confess that I did go through a phase where slicking my hair back, putting on an old dinner jacket, and crooning "Constant Craving" into a hairbrush felt oh-so-right. And sure, many were the times when I pictured myself on stage with Mel, belting out "Bring Me Some Water" while the women in the crowd ripped off their MARTINA FOR ATTORNEY GENERAL T-shirts and flung them at the stage along with the keys to their hotel rooms.

But Wy has something different. She possesses what I call the "I Could Be That Too" quality. She's famous, sure, but she's still one of us. When we listen to her singing, we can imagine ourselves doing the same thing, and it doesn't seem so ridiculous. Why couldn't we have a hit single? Why couldn't we tour the country in a special bus with Clint Black? It doesn't seem so unreasonable. After all, Wynonna did it, and she's just a regular gal who likes Bingo and eating buckets of buffalo wings during the Super Bowl. For heaven's sake, she's even married to a used-car salesman.

Wy isn't, of course, the only celebrity to rise to stardom based on this elusive quality. In fact, American pop culture is crammed with personalities who have done exactly the same thing. Think about it for a minute. Why do millions of people run out and buy Madonna records? Her voice is nothing spectacular. Her acting talent is often at a level below that found in grammar school productions. Without the benefit of makeup artists and hairdressers, she's no great beauty. But we love her madly. And why? Because she looks as though someone snatched her out of a crowd at the mall and made her a star.

In fact, Madonna had her makeover right in front of our very eyes. Remember the early Madonna, a bedraggled, gum-chewing mall rat who pranced around in costumes that looked like something thrown out after a grueling touring season of *Cats* rendered them unfit for use? Millions of girls across America (and some of the boys) saw themselves in her. We copied her hair, her pout, her slutty happiness. In the safety of our bedrooms, we blasted "Burning Up" and "Holiday" while we rolled around on the floor perfecting our stage acts. Then, when the Material Girl cleaned up and made the big time, we all felt as though we'd done it right along with her. As a reward we dubbed her our national heroine.

There's a very good reason we make these people our idols. As Americans we like our art to be nonthreatening. It's true. Mariah Carey and Michael Bolton sell records by the truckful because they don't intimidate anyone. We put them on and sing along, and we know they aren't really any better than we are on our best days. They just have more hair and good remixers. We flock to Tom Cruise and Arnold Schwarzenegger movies not for the challenge or the art, but because we're guaranteed not to have to think about how we're still working in offices with bad lighting or desperately trying to finish our doctoral theses before our funding runs out. And whether we admit it or not, we're all sitting there looking at Tom and Arnold mouthing their insipid dialogue and saying to ourselves, "Yeah, I could do that."

Not that this is a bad thing. If anything, it makes us all feel better about ourselves. Take, for example, Cher. I adore her. So do you, and you know it. It doesn't matter whether Cher is singing, acting, dancing, or pitching hair-care products. She does everything with an air of surprised amusement that the world is letting her get away with it. And we do. We like her because, even if we never get to be as famous as she is, on some level we are all like her. When Meryl Streep wins statue after statue at the Academy Awards, we applaud politely, secretly hating her for her talent and her stupid accents. But when Cher won an Oscar for *Moonstruck,* we went wild. She was every person who ever practiced making an acceptance speech in front of a mirror, and now she had her chance to give our collective thanks. Not only that, but she did it in a dress even Madonna wouldn't have had the balls to wear. More recently Cher was asked to comment on an album she'd just released. Her reply—"I guess it's OK. It doesn't suck."—endeared her to me forever.

On the other hand, while we might respect artists who have undeniably huge amounts of talent, we don't really like them. Yo-Yo Ma may pack Carnegie Hall for his cello recitals, but when's the last time you saw some groupie toss a jockstrap onto the stage at his feet? Sure, there are opera fans who flutter about stage doors like demented moths, but really they're just interested in the sets and costumes. They all know they could never really get onstage at the Met and do *Aida* any justice. And while millions of queens can recite all the lines of every Bette Davis movie, when it comes down to it, none of us wanted to be her friend.

No, we like our *real* stars to maintain a discreet distance. It helps them to generate an aura of otherness that keeps them luminous in our eyes. If they get too close, we scorn them for being mortals like ourselves. Back in Hollywood's golden age, the stars understood this. They secreted themselves behind the walls of their lush estates and engaged in their affairs—both of the heart and of business—far from our prying eyes. From time to time a photo would appear in a magazine or a story would be leaked to the press by a sly publicist. But never the whole thing. We were just given bits and pieces—enough to keep us enthralled but not enough to jeopardize the stars' Olympian status. When they turned out for Oscar night, it was a real event, the gods and goddesses descending to give the mere mortals a glance.

But even then the most popular stars were those who rose from our ranks, the everyday men and especially women plucked from the drudgery of nine-to-five jobs and turned into 20-foot tall giants who strode across the silver screen. We were crazy for plain little Norma Jean Baker, who escaped a troubled marriage and toiled at any number of mundane jobs before dyeing her mouse-brown hair a brilliant platinum and becoming Marilyn, the sexiest woman to ever grace celluloid. And then there was dear Frances Gumm, who transformed herself first into Judy Garland and then into Dorothy Gale, the most beloved movie heroine of all time. Yes, they were ultimately tragic figures, but how many of us watched them and dreamed of sitting at a drugstore soda fountain one minute and being directed by Billy Wilder the next?

Today's stars understand this principle better, perhaps, than their forebears did. They live their lives in the public eye, getting married, having affairs, and breaking up right before our very eyes. Why, we can even buy a video depicting pinup queen Pamela Anderson and rocker husband Tommy Lee doing the nasty, complete with close-ups and come shots. You would never see Myrna Loy or William Powell doing such a thing. But to be popular today, an actor or singer has to let the public know she or he is just one of the gang. Just look at the Spice Girls. While most people would be hard pressed to seriously imagine themselves jamming with the talented but remote Kate Bush, any one of us could become the next Spice Girl. All it takes is an outgoing personality and some fabulous clothes. We appreciate this, and the result is concerts that sell out in 12 seconds flat.

But back to Wynonna. While I love Cher's sheer wildness and the appealing cheekiness of the Spice Girls, Wy is more my style. She doesn't care what she weighs. She doesn't care if the critics like her albums. The people love her, and that's what counts. She looks as though she'd be more than happy to come over and give you a hand with that wallpapering job, and unlike, say, Jewel or Prince, you can easily imagine Wy spending a boring Sunday afternoon parked in front of the television watching Godzilla movies and eating Ben & Jerry's Chocolate Chip Cookie Dough ice cream. Hell, she even signs her name with little musical notes at the end.

It also helps that she sings country music, which is perfect for an "I Could Be That Too" star. When I was a kid, I cringed whenever my father turned the truck radio dial to the country station. There would be Eddie Rabbitt warbling along about loving rainy nights, or Dolly telling the same old story about her coat of many colors. But as I grew older, I found myself listening to it more and more, often surreptitiously. The lyrics were simple and honest, the melodies catchy. These were people like me. Garth Brooks isn't that bad, I'd think to myself, and he's kind of cute. And as for John Michael Montgomery, I secretly bought all of his albums and mooned over his picture.

While I wanted Garth and John Michael to sweep me off my feet, it was Wy I longed to be like, and I still do. Unlike rock music, country is inviting. No matter how polished the sound, it still always comes across as though a bunch of people were sitting around on the porch one night and decided to make a record. And no one is better at putting across that down-home feeling than Wynonna. When she was with her mother, Naomi, and they were simply the Judds, the two of them looked forever like the results of some frightening postseason sale at Kmart. Standing onstage, Naomi with her big doe eyes and Wynonna with her big hair streaked all the wrong shades of blond, they were the embodiment of every wish any of us ever had to be stars. Like escapees from the Barbizon School of Modeling, like *Star Search* gone big time, they took us right along with them.

Now that Wynonna has gone solo, she's even more fabulous. The chubby little girl who got to be homecoming queen, she steadfastly refuses to go home before every cheerleader in the gym cries uncle and admits that she's really cool. Just to prove she knows a thing or two about being the belle of the high school dance, she even recorded a cover of the 1980s adolescent anthem "Free

Bird" on her album *Revelations*. For those of us who endured the playing of this song at the end of every disappointing school dance, Wynonna's rendition has become something of an anthem. Putting it on and singing along, we're instantly transported back to those anxious nights when we stood against the wall, nervously sipping flat Coke while we stared at whatever boy we had a crush on dancing with his girlfriend and prayed no one would notice us. Only now that Wy is in control, he's dancing with us and everyone is jealous.

I used to watch Wynonna strutting around in leather jacket and motorcycle cap and hope she was a dyke. And maybe she is, despite baby and husband. After all, she does drive a Harley. But even if she isn't, I love her just as much. Because if she can do it, so can I. And so can you. In fact, take out those sticks and start practicing your drum licks. I'm going to need a backup band.

Over the Hill

I'll be turning 30 this year. That's 79 in gay years. And I'm not taking it well.

The odd thing is, I've always wanted to be 30. Since about the age of five, I've looked forward to the day when I would hit that milestone. People who were 30 seemed so grown-up to me. So sophisticated and together. I had this idea in my head that on your 30th birthday a delegation arrived at your door and presented you with all the trappings of adulthood, including a car, a fulfilling career, a nurturing relationship, the keys to your own home, and a fully funded IRA.

But here I am only months away, and now I see that I was sadly mistaken. Unless something truly unexpected happens, I will wake up on my big three-oh with no car, no relationship, a far-too-expensive rented apartment, and no financial future whatsoever. OK, so I have something of a career, and on some days it is fulfilling. But I was hoping for more.

I don't know what it is about turning 30 that seems like such a big deal. In fact, when an editor recently rejected a book proposal of mine saying I was too young to be writing it, I stormed around the house for days, furious at her for not recognizing my maturity. "I've written 27 books!" I bellowed at the dog, who yawned and went back to sleep. (He's only four and has no worries.)

Maybe that's the problem. When I was 25 and had

written a handful of books, people were impressed. Editors would phone me and say, "This is amazing for someone your age." My agent couldn't wait to see what I would do next.

But now it's old hat. Why, mere children have written novels these days. Every time I open *The New York Times Book Review,* there's another article about some 20-year-old Columbia student who's published a stunning book about how terrible it is to be young and beautiful. I used to read these pieces and think, *Wait until* my *novel comes out. I'll show them all.*

And I would have shown them—if I'd ever written it. Now it's too late. Now the ideas that would have seemed so smart, so witty, so mature coming from the pen of an undergraduate are merely dull coming from my almost-30 self. Now when I tell people at parties that I'm a writer, they simply yawn and slap another nacho into the ranch dressing when they discover that none of my books have been made into films starring pale boys and English models with hyphenated names.

What's most disturbing to me is that there no longer seem to be gradations of aging. Now you're either in your 20s or you're not. The threshold is getting lower and lower. Once upon a time people in their 30s looked at their 40-something elders and rejoiced that there were a few more plateaus to reach before death. Nowadays anyone over 30 is, well, not 29 anymore. There is the MTV generation, and then there's the rest of us.

I *used* to be a member of the MTV generation. I remember it well. Finally there was a television station that was all about me and the music I listened to. I tuned in and watched as Cyndi Lauper she-bopped across the screen and Billy Idol sneered at the 30-year-olds who dared try to invade his wild territory. Now Billy is well over 30. Cyndi is into her 40s and has a baby. Why, even Madonna is about to hit her 40th. And I can remember when she writhed across the road in "Burning Up" like an eel. I bet she'd break her hip if she tried it now.

I don't know when it happened, but at some point I was sitting in bed watching TV and realized I had the channel on VH1. I did some quick calculations and discovered I hadn't seen MTV in weeks, probably months. I was watching a Stevie Nicks video. They used to show Stevie on MTV. Not anymore. Now everyone I used to watch on that channel has been pushed over to VH1, the channel for "older" viewers.

In defiance I flipped back to MTV. I didn't recognize any of the VJs. When I was younger, they all had names like Martha, J.J., and Nina. Now the place was crawling with kids named things like Kennedy and Carson. They were all pierced and tattooed and surly. Not that I have anything against piercings and tattoos, but back in the old days, that role was reserved for Ricky Rachtman, who hosted the Headbangers Ball at midnight on Saturdays. Now they're everywhere.

Then there was the music. I'm a big music fan, and I used to pride myself on knowing every singer and band out there. I loved them all, from AC/DC to Laura Branigan, Heart to Ozzy Osbourne. I could watch MTV all day and know every word to every song they played. It made my mother crazy. As I sang along with the car radio, she would sigh wearily and wonder out loud why no one liked the New Christy Minstrels these days.

Ha-ha. Now the joke's on me. Now I recognize maybe one out of every 20 artists on MTV. Janet Jackson is easy. But the others confuse me. For one, they all look the same. For another, they all sound the same. I can't tell a Matchbox 20 from a Smash Mouth or a Chumbawamba from a Squirrel Nut Zipper. And who's this Puffy person that keeps stealing other people's songs? In my day anyone called Puffy would have had his ass kicked by Ann and Nancy Wilson from Heart. But now even they're over on VH1, relegated to crooning during the Sunday Brunch segment. Brunch. People in their 20s don't have brunch. Only we old folks do.

It's strange—one day you're the new kids on the block, and the next day you're nothing. Just ask the New Kids on the Block. When they started out they were the same age I was. Now they're all pushing 30, and who gives a damn about any of them? Now it's all about Hanson.

When I was in high school and everyone was talking about what my generation would accomplish, we felt very good indeed. We were the Live Aid generation. We were the space shuttle generation. We were the Rubik's Cube generation. OK, so we didn't actually have anything to do with creating those things, but they represented our youthful vigor and enthusiasm, our cutting-edge possibilities. Now nobody cares. Now it's all about Generation X and what they're up to. And even they're getting nudged aside by their younger siblings. Well, don't look to me for sympathy.

More and more often, I find the phrase "I remember when" creeping into my conversations. This terrifies me. When I was a kid, I cringed whenever one of my parents would start with the "I remember when" stories. They were always things like, "I remember when we had to walk 15 miles to school" or, "I remember when only hookers wore shoes like that." They were things old people said. Tired old people. Not young vibrant people.

Now I'm one of them. I made a list the other day of things that didn't exist when I was a kid. ATMs. The Internet. Alanis Morissette. Why, I can still recall when VCRs were hardly household items. It was a special treat when my father would go to the store and rent one for the weekend. Even then, there were probably only 20 movies to choose from. I recall also the first time I received a bank card. Until then we'd had passbooks. Nobody ever conceived of having machines all over the place that would spit money at you just because you punched in a secret code. As for compact discs, I insisted they were just a fad. And now just a few days ago I heard a 15-year-old say, "Why do they call these record stores? Didn't records disappear, like, years ago?"

My other elderly friends and I now try to outdo one another in this game. "I remember when lunch box thermoses were made of glass," my friend Diane will say. "Yeah, well, I remember when *Saturday Night Live* was funny," our buddy Brian will retort. On and on it goes, with each of us trying to outdo the other in the aging department. I once tried to get them all with, "I remember when we didn't have fire," but their faculties aren't that far gone that they would buy it. Maybe next year.

This whole gay thing doesn't help matters, either. If I were straight, I'd worry about not yet having made partner or my first million or any number of ridiculous things. But being a queer man, all of those failures pale in comparison to the biggest one of all—I can no longer be the boy of the moment.

Once upon a time I looked forward to being the object of lust of men everywhere, at least men older than myself, men who would do things like fly me to Paris for the weekend and use me as a decorative object near their swimming pools. Never mind that it would be shallow and empty; it would be fun. When I turned 30 I could at least sigh and remember fondly the year I was 23 and the count threw me a party at his palace where we all danced naked in the fountain and fed one another grapes.

Somehow, though, it all passed me by. Maybe I was too busy writing all those books. Maybe I was just too tired. Whatever the reason, I've quietly slipped past the point where anyone is going to call me "that handsome young man" and pine longingly for me. Now I find myself futilely eyeing the 19-year-old stock boys at Stop &

Shop as I pile frozen burritos into my cart and hope the night will bring a Discovery Channel documentary about the feeding habits of sharks.

I know in my heart that 30 is really just the beginning. But not everyone seems to agree with me, and that makes it hard. I opened a book a couple of months ago, a gay novel that was being touted as a masterfully crafted look at gay middle age. The opening scene has the protagonist watching a group of men dancing in a bar. He has his eye on one of them, but fears the boy won't have any interest in him because of his advanced age. A few pages later we discover that the narrator is something like 32. Thirty-two! Only three years older than myself.

When I was first coming out, I always dated "older" men. Now I've become one of those men. I realized this one night when a visiting friend of mine invited me out to meet up with some of his other friends. When we arrived at the appointed restaurant, I found myself sitting at a table with a group of other men around my age. One of the men had with him a young man he had recently started dating. The boy was 21 and recently out himself.

As the evening progressed I watched this young man. He stayed silent as he listened to what we were talking about. When dinner arrived—sushi—his companion had to explain to him what sushi was and how it is eaten. As I watched him fumbling with his chopsticks and taking his first tentative bite from a piece of tuna sushi, I had the sudden realization that he was looking at all of us the way I had looked at the older men who took me under their wings when I was his age. He was watching our faces and, I could tell, wondering what his life would be like when he was as old as we were. I had to resist the urge to tell him.

At least I can take heart in the fact that I am not the only gay man to feel the effects of the big three-oh. A few days ago I was complaining to my friend Tom, newly

30'd, about my dismal romantic possibilities. "Don't even start," he said. "Last week I had my first sexual experience where someone called me 'daddy.' I pictured my father and immediately lost my erection."

"Just be glad he didn't call you 'ma'am,'" I told him wearily.

At our age you have to count your blessings.

A Taxing Time

It happens every year, as inevitably as the post-Christmas blues or Dick Clark's New Year's Rockin' Eve. Before I've recovered from all of the holiday food I've eaten, before I've even begun to get a start on breaking all of my newly made resolutions, the telephone rings.

"Hello?"

"Hi, Mike, it's Wayne."

My accountant. It's tax time again. Like a heat wave come to melt the snowman in my yard, Wayne has arrived to crush any happy thoughts I might have about beginning a new year with a fresh start. But he has his reasons for calling so soon after the turning of the calendar. Even though they aren't due until April, we always start my taxes as early as possible because, after several years of working together, Wayne knows what's in store for him.

The problem is that I resent paying taxes. Because I'm a writer, every cent I earn comes from something I spend a lot of time working on. It's not like I have a job, where I could sit around playing solitaire on my computer for three hours and still collect a paycheck. If I don't write, I don't get paid. Like Donna Summer, I work hard for the money, and I want to keep it. All of it.

Besides, it's not like I'm getting anything for my tax dollars. I don't use the public schools or libraries. At the rate things are going, I'll never see my Social Security benefits. I have never been the beneficiary of federal disaster relief because my house was burned up by a volcano or washed away by a flood. Nor am I particularly cheered to know that my tax contribution helped pay for yet another missile launcher or that it bought a group of overweight and underworked congresspeople a nice lunch or that it funded some high school dropout's stay at boot camp. Even when I go to the public park, which I help pay for, no one comes and picks up after my dog for me. I have to do it myself.

Because I can't take out my frustrations on the government—there being hefty fines for writing "Bite me!" in the margins of one's tax return—I do the next best thing. I take it out on Wayne. As a representative of the entire system, and as someone who makes a living off of perpetuating the horror of taxes, I feel he should have to be at least a little bit responsible for the misery it all brings me. It's only fair.

Besides, he has to put up with it because I pay him. From what I understand, there are now clever computer programs that do in 12 seconds what it seems to take accountants three weeks to do. I probably should get one and save myself the money I pay Wayne every spring. But you can't really yell at a computer program. Well, you can, but when you do you don't get the pleasure of watching it start to sweat. So I stick with Wayne.

Let me make it clear that I do not physically abuse Wayne in any way. That would be too easy. The way I get my revenge is through my itemized deductions. I claim absolutely everything. The problem is, these kinds of things are gigantic red flags for the little tax gremlins who decide which returns to audit. They already hate freelance writers, because we have better jobs than they do and rarely have proof of income, so they delight in anything they can use against us to make our lives miserable. Therefore, itemized deductions make accountants like

Wayne very nervous, and I arrive with piles of them.

"How could you possibly have spent $7,629 on office supplies?" Wayne bellows when I arrive at his office a week after his phone call and dump a pile of receipts on his desk.

"Easy," I say. "Groceries."

"You can't deduct food," he says firmly.

I fix him with a stare. "If I don't have groceries, I can't eat. And if I can't eat, I can't write. Therefore, groceries are a necessary office supply."

Wayne grits his teeth. It's early in the game, and he knows from experience to save his strength. "Fine. But what about this one. Seven hundred dollars on donations? I know you—you don't give money to anyone."

"I donated it to myself," I say, as though speaking to a small child. "So I could afford to keep writing. Think of it as an artistic grant. They can't tax those."

This is true, even if my logic is a bit shaky. We move on. "Three hundred dollars in medical expenses?"

"Roger's vet bills," I explain easily. "From when he swallowed all that string and had to have it removed. He can't get insurance, you know."

By now Wayne is whimpering softly. He's been through audits with other clients, and he knows the government's policy on pet care: Zero Tolerance.

"At least I didn't claim him as a dependent like I did last year," I remind him. "I *could* have deducted another $530 in dog food bills and another $123 for squeaky toys."

He ignores me. "I suppose you have a good excuse for this $1250 business trip?"

"Of course," I say. "That's my trip to Jamaica."

He brightens. "Oh, so you went to a writers conference? Conference expenses are definitely legitimate." He starts to make a note on my form, thrilled that at last I have a legitimate deductible expense.

"No," I say, feeling only slightly guilty at breaking his

bubble. "I went and lay in the sun and had someone bring me fruit drinks."

"You can't deduct that!" he shrieks, his face turning bright red. "It's not business!"

"But I *thought* about writing," I tell him patiently. "Surely that has to count for something. If I can't think about it, I can't write it. And I did read the new Joan Collins novel. Isn't that research or something?"

"They don't see it that way," Wayne says, covering his face with his hands.

After a moment of silence and a deep swig from the Pepto-Bismol bottle on his desk, we continue with my list. Wayne balks at my $430 for magazines (I *insist* that *Vanity Fair* is a trade journal), $1,174 in office renovations (the new oak floors are very nice), and the $2,387 for work-related clothing ("Do you want me to write *naked*?") stops him cold.

I win each of our battles, but having to constantly explain to Wayne why it is perfectly reasonable to claim $670 in gym fees, $320 for my annual Christmas party, and $976.32 in 900-number phone calls is not as fun as it was two hours earlier. We are both relieved when he finally gets to the last item on my list.

"I absolutely refuse to let you deduct the $47 you spent on my Christmas gift," he says in his best accountant voice. "That definitely does not count as a writing expense. And after what you put me through every year..."

"OK," I say, eager to get out of his office and deciding to give him one so he feels he's accomplished something. "I guess that really doesn't have anything to do with writing."

He grins triumphantly and begins to cross it off.

Then I have a thought. "But what if I do a column about it?"

Game, Set, Contract

I hate suspense. Really I do. I like to know what is going to happen at all times and to whom, especially if it is me. I do not enjoy movies where people/animals/aliens pop out from behind/under/on top of anything in order to provide an element of surprise. I stay away from amusement park rides that think they are whimsical because they turn a corner and drop the rider 3,000 feet, screaming, into a pool of water. I do not think talk shows in which guests are presented with their secret crushes are at all fun.

This loathing for not knowing what will happen carries over into my everyday life. I like to know what's waiting a few weeks or months down the line. Unlike some of my acquaintances, who find it thrilling to live from moment to moment in the belief that *anything* can happen, I like to know what I will be doing six months from now. I schedule writing projects a year ahead of time. I make dinner arrangements for New Year's on January 2. I already have plans for my 40th birthday, even though it's a decade away.

Like many people, I have my own superstitions and ways of foretelling the future. But not for me are the usual routes of tarot cards or palm readers. No, the crystal balls and magic mirrors into which I peer are awards shows and sporting events. On the surface these two things have very little in common with one another. But for me, they share a common bond. I am addicted to both of these things. And for the same reason, I want the people I like to win because I am convinced it will have a direct influence on my life.

Much as my ancestors rummaged through the entrails of fish and scanned the heavens for signs of impending doom or good fortune, I fully believe that my well-being hinges squarely on whether or not, say, the Boston Bruins make it to the Stanley Cup finals. Similarly, I view awards shows as a fortune-teller might look at a tarot spread. If the right person wins, then my novel in progress will be a success. If the envelope contains the name of the wrong nominee, then I might as well forget it.

Stop laughing. It's true, and I can prove it. It all started a few years ago, when little Anna Paquin was nominated for a best supporting actress Oscar for her work in *The Piano*. I desperately wanted her to win because I figured anyone who had to be in the proximity of Harvey Keitel's naked weenie deserved something to take home. But Anna was a long shot. For weeks I agonized over this. At the same time I was also agonizing over the draft of a book I needed to sell. The two became as one; if Anna took home Oscar, my book would fly.

The night of the ceremonies, I was a wreck. I loaded up on Cheetos and Ovaltine, watching as envelope after envelope was opened. Finally, it was time to reveal the best supporting actress. Each nominee was announced. Close-ups of expectant faces were arranged on the screen like a grim family tree. The presenter slid his finger under the envelope flap.

And I changed the channel.

This is the problem with my method. While I rely heavily on the outcome of such things, I cannot bring myself to actually watch the moments when they arrive. It's simply too much pressure. I have so much riding on what happens that to watch it unfold would make me insane. I prefer instead to let it all happen offscreen and then tune in for the deciding moment when I can see at a glance whether my champion has won or lost.

I flipped back to the Oscars a few seconds later, only to see Anna standing triumphant, her chubby cheeks bright with surprise. I couldn't believe it. Against the odds, she had won. I collapsed onto the bed and wept. The next day I sold my book for a hefty sum. Scoff if you will, but Anna Paquin is probably the only nine-year-old actress with a novel dedicated to her.

Since then I have used awards shows and sporting events many times as indicators of my future. When Alanis Morissette walked off with an armful of Grammys, the man I'd been lusting after for months asked me out. A week later the Red Sox were beaten bitterly and I discovered he was married. Even Miss America is fair game. When my favorite, Miss North Dakota, came in second to Miss Texas, my next royalty check was paltry indeed. So it goes.

But as monumental as these moments are, I can't actually watch them, much as I'd like to. "Why did you flip away?" my friends scream as the best picture is announced.

"If it's *Braveheart,* I'll never get that grant!" I wail. And I didn't. Blame it all on Mel Gibson.

Tennis is the worst. I love to watch it, especially women's tennis, but it gets me so keyed up I feel my heart beating irregularly. Unlike in other sports, the balance of power in tennis changes from one shot to the next, and the outcome is dependent solely on the activity of the two players, not on a team. If one falters, the wrong person can sneak up and win just like that. Also, the score has to be played out over several sets, not just one long match, so a winning player can suddenly find herself on the ropes. Winning or losing a match can easily result from one single service break, making watching an entire three-set match an excruciating experience.

Take, for example, the 1996 U.S. Open. During its two-week run, I had a novel sitting with an agent I very much wanted to take me on as a client. As far as I was concerned, she was the *only* agent who could make me a star and bring me the wealth that had for so long eluded me. I decided that if Monica Seles, whom I had been feeling kindly toward in recent weeks, won the tournament, the agent would adore me. If she lost, it was back to the salt mines.

Now, some people would say that I can have undue influence on my fate by choosing people I know will win. I beg to differ. I admit that there's a marked difference between pinning one's hopes on Monica Seles and someone like, say, the sure-to-choke Jana Novotna. (OK, Novotna won Wimbledon in 1998, but she's still the reigning queen of choke.) But my choice was not without risks. Even though Monica had been playing well, a win at the Open was not assured for her. She was still dealing with the death of her father, and the pressure of returning to the game after being stabbed by a disturbed Graf fan almost two years earlier.

Then there was the little matter of Steffi Graf. Now, I appreciate Steffi Graf. I know it must be very difficult to continue to be at the top of the heap while your father is sitting in prison. And she is a marvelous player. But I don't like her. I'm sorry. I just don't. People who are that good for so long are just tiresome, as they make the rest of us feel fat and undermotivated. Since her return, Monica had been sharing the number one spot with Steffi. Since the two were seeded number one and two at the Open and thus could meet only in the final, I was praying that Monica would get the chance to kick her ass and take over as queen of the court. Thus it was with these many expectations that I began the two-week wait to see what my fate would be.

The first week was fairly easy. Monica breezed through her early rounds without so much as breaking a sweat. I thought happy thoughts about my book and waited for week two. This was tougher, but I did it. I watched nervously as Monica whacked her way through the quarterfinals against Amanda Coetzer, who had been having the tournament of her life. Despite aggravating her sore shoulder, Monica came through, though I had to see match point on a replay because I was about to throw up from the tension.

The semifinal match against Conchita Martinez was harder to stomach. Although I knew Conchita had never beaten Monica in all of their meetings, Seles seemed a little under the weather as she took the court in a drizzle brought about by Hurricane Fran, which had recently demolished the Carolinas. Luckily for me, she didn't hold back. The first sent went by quickly, and although there was a sticky point in the second where Monica failed on six break points, eventually Conchita went down like a Spanish galleon on fire.

That meant there was only one more match standing between Monica and a Grand Slam victory and me and a new agent. And the woman blocking the way was none other than Steffi Graf. Secretly, I had been hoping that some young upstart would have knocked a surprised Graf out of the competition, thus almost assuring Monica of victory. But like some dark vulture circling my life, Steffi had hung in and gotten to the end.

So on the day of the final, there I sat, a bag of Oreos in my lap to distract me from the match. I made it through the first few games without fear, as both players performed their usual tricks and held serve. Then, in the fifth game, Steffi turned up the heat. Monica faltered and lost serve. Steffi held and won the set.

Tension comes immediately in a women's match because women play only three sets (whereas men play five). Consequently, there's little room for error. Andre Agassi can lose the first set and not feel pressured. But when a woman drops the first set, she is immediately pitched into a battle for her life. Poor Monica was facing another tournament loss, and we were only half an hour into the match. I shoved a handful of Oreos into my mouth and watched the second set.

After 35 minutes and half a bag of cookies, Monica had evened the match at one set apiece, and now the pressure was on both players. Should Monica win, she would claim her first Grand Slam title since the stabbing. She would also give Steffi a good swift kick in the pants. And I'd have an agent. As the ball went up to begin the third and final set, I grew tense. Well, more tense than before.

Both players held serve, battling fiercely for every point. Neither was giving in. Then, finally, Monica had a break opportunity. In fact, she had three chances to take a game away from her opponent and forge ahead by one critical break. No problem, I thought confidently. This is it. Monica would get her break. And once she had it, she'd win. I was sure of it. I thought about my new agent and smiled happily.

Steffi served the first break chance. And got an ace. Not to worry, I thought, there are still two more. But then the second break chance went up in smoke as Monica returned the serve directly into the net. I began to worry. But she still had one break chance left. Surely she wouldn't let it slip away.

Steffi stood across the net, glaring Teutonically, and prepared to serve. Determined to break my pattern of turning away and not watching the outcome, I hid the remote control under the couch and kept my eyes on the screen. Steffi served, and the ball went screaming towards Monica. She returned it with a solid *thwack*!

"Eat felt, you bitch!" I screamed at Steffi, sending the

dog scurrying from the room in terror.

But Steffi didn't eat felt. Instead, she sent the ball whizzing past a startled Monica with a searing cross-court forehand. Monica stood, dazed, as the ball miraculously landed neatly on the chalk line and bounded teasingly away. I could see the disappointment in her eyes. I could feel mine in my stomach, which was churning with Oreos and anticipation.

It was all over after that. Steffi, encouraged by her save, went on to win the game. She then broke Monica three times in a row and prepared to serve for the tournament. Monica looked whipped. So did I. Even downing the rest of the bag of Oreos didn't help. I tried to change the channel, but I'd managed to hide the remote so well that I couldn't find it. Too distraught to get up and turn the TV off, I lay there in a defeated pile as Steffi won championship number 3,907 or something like that.

During the awards ceremony, Steffi beamed and held her gleaming trophy aloft as though she'd just miraculously pulled a child out of a well and wanted to show it off to the assembled crowd. Monica gamely hoisted her pathetic second-place plate and smiled wanly as storm clouds covered the sun and dulled the silver a joyless gray. I could tell she wanted to hit Steffi over the head with it.

An hour later, the mail came to my house. In it was a letter from the agent I'd sent my manuscript to. I didn't even have to open it. Monica's face had shown me everything I needed to know. We were both losers, and it was all Steffi Graf's fault.

Still, I continue to scan the television for signs of hope. A few weeks after the U.S. Open, Helen Hunt won an Emmy and I sold a short story. Now I'm trying another agent with my manuscript. All I can say is, the Red Sox better win the Series.

My Life in Reviews

I have written a lot of books in a lot of different genres. I've published very serious nonfiction, novels, and even a couple of erotica titles. I've written for children and adults, straight readers and queer readers. But whatever the book, and whatever the audience, the process of getting the book out into the world is pretty much the same.

The publication of a new book is indeed a thrilling time. After all, generally you've worked very hard and spent a lot of time writing the thing and nagging the publisher about what you think the cover should look like and about how this time they really should send you around the country on a reading tour, just like Anne Rice. As the publication date approaches, you spend every waking moment hovering near the front door, waiting for the UPS guy to pull up with the package containing your free author copies.

When he finally arrives you can't open the box fast enough and get your hands on your new baby. After checking to make sure it has all of its fingers and toes, you call everyone you've ever met in your entire life, just to say hello, of course, but maybe somewhere in the conversation you can slip it in that you happen to have a new book out and that if your friend really likes you, she'll go out and buy a copy immediately.

For a couple of weeks, everything is sweetness and

light. Your friends all tell you how wonderful and fabulous the book is and how no one will possibly notice the glaring typo on page 97 where it says "pubic" instead of "public." You call your editor and tell him how much fun it was to work with him, even though three months ago you were calling him the dumbest son of a bitch to ever wield a red pencil. You put the book somewhere where you can see it every time you happen to walk by. Sometimes you pick it up and read a few pages, pretending it's someone else's book and wishing you could write so well. Then you remember that you *did* write it, and you sigh happily at your brilliance and wait for the phone to ring again.

But lurking on the horizon is a dark cloud that threatens to ruin the sunny joy of your publication experience. Like a sharp-toothed and hungry shark lurking just below the crystal-blue waters of your happiness is the one thing that could possibly turn your dream come true into a nightmare—the reviews. See, your friends and loved ones aren't the only ones who are allowed to comment on your book. Unfortunately, just about everyone is allowed to say whatever they want to about what you've written. This being America, there aren't laws to stop them, which is really something that needs to be addressed by Congress.

OK, so usually it isn't that terrible. I've written almost 30 books, and in general they've been very well reviewed. In fact, out of all of the reviews I've ever gotten, only two have been the really awful kind that make me go to bed for a week and wonder if I'll have to get a real job now. And those were written by insignificant little people who will certainly never write books of their own and whose names I can no longer remember, probably because I burned their nasty little scraps of viciousness. I admit, however, that while I can recall very little of the positive reviews, I remember nearly every word of those two bad ones. No, I won't tell you what they said.

I suspect I am like most writers in how I approach reading my reviews. Instead of starting at the beginning and jumping right in, I scan the lines quickly. The purpose of this is to look for key words. If among the jumble of words that flash by my eye registers such phrases as "delightfully funny" and "Nobel Prize," then chances are good that reading the review slowly will make me happy. But should I come across something along the lines of "disappointing" or "don't bother because this book is about the dumbest piece of crap ever published," then I begin to suspect that experiencing the review in its entirety will bring me little joy.

You would think at that point I would simply close the magazine or newspaper and do something more pleasant. But I don't. No matter how awful it might be, I find myself compelled to read every single word of every review. If the review is a positive one, I assume the writer is correct and that my material is all the wonderful things she says it is. If it's not so nice, then I have to take more time, because I'm forced to ascribe motivation to the negativity of the author. This could be anything from simple jealousy to the possibility that he broke up with his boyfriend moments before reading my book and felt the need to take it out on me.

Even with bad reviews, however, there are ways to turn them into something positive. No, I do not mean by looking at them objectively, taking them to heart, and seeing what I might possibly do differently in my next book. I mean by rewriting them.

The first time a less-than-flattering review came in for a book I'd published, I called the editor to whine about how unfair it was. There was no way we could use the quotes in ads for the book or on the cover of the paperback when it came out. At least that's what I thought. But then she showed me something magical, something

I would never have thought of on my own. See, you don't have to use entire sentences when quoting from reviews. You can just use the nice words.

For example, if the review says, "This ambitious but insipid book will appeal only to everyone who thinks *Melrose Place* is high cinema and believes that everything by Jackie Collins is a masterpiece," there is no need to weep. With just the tiniest bit of editing, you end up with, "This ambitious...book will appeal to everyone ...and...is a masterpiece."

OK, so maybe it looks a little weird. But when it's set in type and surrounded by lots of design elements, it looks fine. No one will notice the herd of ellipses trampling through the quote, and with a little luck everyone will think that you cut some stuff out because it was so laudatory that even you were embarrassed by it. The point is: If you read it enough, even you will come to believe that it's what the reviewer actually meant to say. And that's what's really important, isn't it? Happiness, after all, is all about perception.

While this little trick is indeed miraculous, its true implications reach far beyond the field of literature. It has many practical applications in our everyday lives, and I think it's high time we adopted it for everyday use.

For example, feel free to use it any time someone gives you news you don't want to hear. Say the object of your six-month obsession turns down your offer of a date, saying, "I can't go out with you because I'm much better-looking and because you're a pathetic loser and really don't deserve great sex with someone like me." Don't feel bad. Just turn it into, "I can't go out with you because I'm...a pathetic loser and...don't deserve great sex." See, it's easy. And fun. With a little practice, your life will be nothing but rave reviews.

Editing out the unpleasant portions of your life comes in especially handy when dealing with family members who might historically have been thorns in your side. Now, I'm not implying that *all* mothers are prone to fits of nagging, but let's just say that more than a few of my friends have adapted the cut-and-paste method of viewing reality when coping with the sometimes stressful process of maternal relationships.

"It was just fabulous," said my friend Janet over dinner last night. I had recently told her about my new way of looking at the world and urged her to try it for herself. "My mother called last night like she always does. And of course she started in about how I'm wasting my life being a lesbian. You know, the usual 'How can you be happy when you're an outcast' crap."

"So what did you do?" I asked, curious to hear how she'd fared.

"Well," said Janet. "At one point she said, 'Your father and I have accepted that we'll never have grandchildren, but we'd really appreciate it if you could try not to flaunt your lifestyle in our faces every time we see you.' I just nipped and tucked and had her saying, 'Your father and I have accepted and appreciate your lifestyle.' It was a turning point in our relationship."

We clinked glasses in a toast to Janet's newfound editing skills. But her triumph was nothing compared to what my friend Barry managed to do a couple of days later.

"Look at this," he said when I answered the door. He was holding a piece of paper, which he shoved into my hand.

"What is it?" I asked.

"Just read," he said, grinning from ear to ear.

On one side of the paper was a speech that had been given by a member of Congress regarding gay pride celebrations. It read, in part, "It is a well-documented fact that the majority of American citizens are God-fearing people who do not condone the outrageous antics of sodomites. They do not want to be forced to look at these deviants who flaunt their unholy lifestyles by parading around in leather underwear and riding topless down our streets in yearly orgies of self-indulgence. It's high time we stop talking nonsense about special rights and put the interests of our children first by helping communities keep themselves clean of such filth and stopping the perverts who insist it is somehow their right to corrupt their young minds."

Barry had unraveled this tangle of bigoted nonsense and, using only the barest minimum of dots, come up with the far more truthful and amusing rendition of the facts: "It is a well-documented fact that the majority of American citizens are...sodomites...who flaunt their ...lifestyles by parading around in leather underwear. It's high time we...put the interests of our children first by helping communities...corrupt their young minds."

"Now if we could just get him to read our version," I told Barry when I'd finished reading his new and improved version.

"We might get our chance," he said. "I'm dating his speechwriter."

See, this whole thing has enormous potential. In this day of computer editing and photo manipulation, there's no reason why we can't take the words of our oppressors and turn them against them. By cutting out all of the extraneous stuff that hides their true meanings, we can reveal them for the dunces that they are.

As for me, I have a new book out soon, and I'm ready to go through the whole publishing process again. If you're a reviewer, take a look at the book. If you like it, that's great. You're a fabulous person whose mother brought you up right. If you don't, just remember—I'm sitting here with scissors in hand.

Part Four

God Is Dog
Spelled Backward

Man's Best Friend

There's no denying it—I will never have a boyfriend. No, I haven't given up on men or decided that going straight is the answer. Nor have I fallen in with an obscure alien-loving cult that demands my celibacy as part of their plan to lure the Mother Ship back to Earth. It's just that there's no room in the bed.

The bed is big enough. Queen size, in fact. When I first got it, I looked at the vast expanse of space and imagined hours of sweaty fun rolling around on the rumpled sheets with whatever man I could lure into my bedroom. It was my first grown-up bed, and I was looking forward to sleeping on something that did not cleverly convert into a couch during the daytime hours.

Then the dog wandered in. He took one look at the new purchase and jumped up on it. After bouncing a few times to test the spring in the mattress, he plopped himself down for a nap.

He hasn't moved since. In fact, as time has gone on he's taken over more and more of the bed for his own, until now all I get is a thin strip along the right edge. Like some kind of bed-space refugee, I lie on my side at night in this no-man's-land, trying to pull enough of the quilt over me to keep warm and wondering where I went wrong.

I admit that it's probably all my fault. After all, when Roger first started getting on the bed, it crossed my mind that perhaps it wasn't such a good idea. And all of the dog books I'd bought said it was a definite no-no to allow pets on the furniture. But he was a puppy at the time, and he looked so cute curled up in a little black Labrador ball with his nose on his paws. Besides, he didn't take up that much space, and it was sort of cozy to feel him beside me at night.

But now Roger weighs 110 pounds and is as long as I am tall. And while he still sometimes sleeps curled up in a ball, more often he stretches out as much as he can. His favorite position is on his back with his head on the pillows and all four legs straight up in the air. More than once I've been rudely awakened by a paw being forced into my lower back as Roger decides that he would be a lot more comfortable if I moved over just a little bit.

Even his bed-hogging activities wouldn't bother me so much if it weren't for the sand. Labradors like nothing better than swimming, and Roger swims daily, even in winter. Somehow, along with the water in the pond, he manages to soak up vast quantities of sand, all of which he immediately deposits on the bed when he gets home. It's like sleeping in the Sahara. Last week I put on newly washed sheets. When I went to bed, I slipped beneath them, thrilled to be surrounded by material that didn't smell like wet dog or abrade my skin.

My joy lasted for approximately 20 seconds. Then Roger came bounding in, leaped up onto the bed, and lay down. The next thing I knew, I felt sand on my legs. Then came the overwhelming smell of the great outdoors. Roger let out a happy groan, rolled onto his back, and started to snore as I thought about the average life span of Labradors and wept, realizing I'll be at least 40 before I get my bed back.

I know what you're thinking: Why don't you just kick him off? Anyone who would say that has clearly never owned a dog, especially not a manipulative

Labrador. I *have* tried to make him sleep on the floor. He even has his very own cedar-filled bed from L.L. Bean. Every so often, when I'm particularly tired of the sand and the dog smell, I tell him to sleep on it. He dutifully gets down, goes to the bed, and spends 20 minutes pawing at the stuffing until he has it all fluffed up the way he wants it. Then he throws himself down on it, and I try to go to sleep.

About three minutes later, the sighing begins. No one is a bigger drama queen than Roger, and he has a way of pushing out air that makes him sound like the world's most deprived animal. No matter how hard I try to ignore him, I can feel him there on the floor, staring at me in the big warm bed while he sleeps on the cold L.L. Bean doggie pillow, and I can't stand it. He hears my resolve shatter, and up he comes, settling down with a contented sigh.

Things have gotten so bad that when Roger pulled a muscle in his back a couple of months ago and couldn't climb the stairs, let alone jump onto the bed, I was forced to bring everything down to his level. Instead of accepting that he would have to sleep on his own bed for a few weeks while he recuperated, he cried until I took the big bed apart and laid the mattress on the floor. Once it was there, he wagged his tail happily and stepped onto his newly lowered mattress. Digging at the quilt until he had it balled up just the way he likes it, he settled down as if he'd known all along that this was how things would turn out.

I'm not the only one suffering from this dog-in-the-bed syndrome. My friend Diane is too. Her Dalmatian, Rudy, also sleeps on the bed. And not just *on* the bed. Rudy actually sleeps *in* the bed, right there underneath all the sheets and blankets. More than once, a startled partner has felt her toes being sucked in the middle of the night, only to discover that the guilty party isn't

Diane but her spotted other half. The relationship seldom proceeds any further.

Every night, while other people are going out on dates and thinking about all the fun they'll have later on in their dog-free beds, Diane and I walk Roger and Rudy around the pond. As our happy pets romp and play, we wearily trudge along behind them, wondering if maybe somewhere out there are people who might not mind sleeping with big dogs between us and them. But we doubt it.

Besides, we have enough trouble with the dogs in our lives. Adding other people to it would simply be too exhausting. As it is, I take Roger out five or six times a day. That doesn't include the car rides, the midnight outings to look for the skunk that lives behind the house, or the trips to the vet to find out why he's throwing up again. I don't have time to date anyone. What little free time I have is spent washing Roger's blankets and planning his birthday parties.

I've developed a theory about all of this. I think that in his former life Roger was a Tibetan monk, perhaps even a Dalai Lama. I know Buddhist tradition dictates that souls generally progress upward, but what could be better than being a dog who gets every comfort he desires? And what more could a weary monk who lived a life of hardship look forward to than a nice cushy bed and someone to rub his ears whenever he wants? Watching Roger smile in his sleep, or waiting for him while he has one of his endless sniffing moments during a walk, I can't help but wonder if somewhere, somehow, hundreds of years ago, he and I didn't live as teacher and pupil, and now we're just doing it all over again.

Usually I feel privileged to have such experiences. But sometimes it gets to be a little much. A few nights ago, after calculating the exact length of time it's been since anyone but Roger and I have shared my bed, I decided enough was enough. Marching into the bedroom, I was determined to toss Roger off the bed once and for all.

But when I went in, he was curled up in a ball. His head was on the pillow, and in his paws he was holding his favorite stuffed toy, a polar bear named Bruce. I stood there for a minute, looking down at my sleeping, stinking monster. Then I got in next to him, pulled the little bit of the blanket not already around him over me, and turned off the light.

Oh, My God

I've known God for a long time. Almost for a quarter of a century now. Granted, that's nothing compared to how long he's been around, but I do think it's long enough to have formed some opinions about him and gotten some insights into his behavior. And it's certainly longer than I've known any of my other friends.

I first met God when my mother introduced us. I must have been about three or four, and she said she had a good friend she wanted me to meet. Always up for getting to know new people, I told her to set something up. I was a little dismayed when she explained that I couldn't see or hear him, making lunch or drinks out of the question, but I was trusting enough to believe her when she said he'd listen to me if I talked to him. It was, to my mind, kind of like having an invisible friend. When she informed me that he'd actually created the whole world, I was very impressed indeed. None of my other friends had accomplished much beyond being able to tie their shoes or make it through the night dry.

To tell the truth, I was a little afraid that he wouldn't be interested in me. After all, what had I done to equal his feats of greatness? But I went ahead and met him. And at first things went smoothly, despite our considerable age difference. I talked to God frequently, and as far as I knew, he heard me. He didn't ask for anything, and that suited me just fine. I didn't have a lot to give anyway, being that I was just starting to figure out who I was. I was proud to have such an important friend on my side so early in life. To be sure, I didn't know much about him, but he seemed like a nice enough fellow—sort of like the grandfather I'd never had. Besides, he kept the monsters away while I slept, and for that I was thankful.

Then, a few years after I first met God, I started to learn some things about him that troubled me. According to my Sunday School teacher, who claimed to have known God for much longer than I had, he wasn't always the pleasant, fun-loving guy I'd been led to believe he was. In fact, according to her side of the story, he could sometimes get so mad that he would actually destroy everything he'd created, including people who got in his way. She even had proof, and she showed me, in black and white, just what he was capable of. Of course, he'd promised to never do it again, but things just weren't the same after that. I mean, if he'd kept the destruction of the world a secret, who knew what else he might be hiding from me.

Curious to see what else I didn't know about my friend, I began to read up on God and his past. Luckily, there was a lot of information. Imagine my shock when I discovered that in addition to flooding the earth, he'd also been known to level whole cities, turn people into salt, smite entire armies, and cause men to become covered in boils, all just for crossing him. Sure, he always said he had a good reason, but I'd been around enough to know that every kid on the playground with a penchant for biting or hair-pulling could and nearly always did claim to have been provoked. I was tempted to confront God head-on about all of these things, but given his past behavior, I wasn't sure I wanted to get on his bad side, so I kept quiet and pretended everything was fine.

For a couple of years after my discoveries, God and I had an uneasy relationship. Firmly believing that people can change if they want to, I was unwilling to cut him out of my life forever because of some past mistakes. Besides, that had all been a long time ago. As far as I knew, he'd been pretty good for the last century or so. I still asked him to watch over my grandparents and my dog, and he seemed to be doing a fine job.

But still I had doubts. I wasn't sure I entirely believed his claims of greatness. Surely someone who had created the heavens and the earth could get me a new skateboard for my birthday, but it never seemed to happen. Growing disillusioned, I started to talk to him less and less, and wondered if he even noticed. I continued to show up for his birthday party every year, but more and more it was just for the cake and the favors than for him. Some years I didn't even bring a present.

Things grew more strained when I became an adolescent and started to ask harder questions. No longer content to believe in anything just because someone told me to, God became in my mind a kind of cosmic Puff the Magic Dragon. Without hard proof, I wasn't going to be so quick to accept his extravagant claims. Why, I demanded to know, would someone create an entire world and then let bad things like war and disease loose upon it? If God was so great, how come things sucked so bad? Gone was the benevolent old man of my childhood. God had become more like the Joker on *Batman,* looking on as we squirmed helplessly below him. Angered, I stopped talking to him altogether and sat in my room alone, listening to AC/DC, which I knew he hated.

My mother tried to patch things up between us. "Don't be so hard on him," she said. "He's just doing his job. And all of those bad things, well, they're just tests for us to see how much we really believe in him. Wars, famine, death—they're all our fault, not God's. If we believed in him, they'd never happen. He's really a nice guy. Besides, he misses you. Give him another chance."

OK, I thought, maybe she's right. Reluctantly, I decided to mend fences. After being out of touch for a while, I went back to talking to God. At first it was tentative—a brief hello here and there, a short talk before a big math test. Like schoolgirls making up after a fight, we eased back into it, until finally one afternoon I asked him if he'd like to come over. We stayed up all night talking, and in the morning it was as though we'd never fought. Soon we were doing everything together, ignoring our other friends for one another's company.

We spent all of our time together. I even, for one long summer, became a missionary for him, traveling to France with a group of other young people to spread his word. It was like falling in love, and I was hooked. All I wanted to do was hold God's hand and surprise him with little gifts. I just knew he liked me better than the others, and I had to admit, I'd missed him.

Besides, I was learning a great deal about the world by dating an older man, especially one who'd created it in the first place. Plus, things seemed so much easier when all I had to do to answer a question was open up a book and see what God had to say about it. He seemed to know everything. Excited by our new friendship, I tried to introduce my friends to God too and pitied them when they refused to invite him to their parties. I knew they just couldn't accept our relationship.

Once again, things went on happily for a time. All throughout high school we stayed together. We made a good couple, even if he couldn't take me to any of the dances. Then, in my final year (actually my junior year, as I dropped out my senior year), our relationship hit another bump in the road. Maybe he'd kept me waiting one too many times. Maybe as we both aged we'd just outgrown one another. Whatever the reason, one day I found myself wondering: What kind of person was God if he'd create people without ever asking their permission and then threaten to send them to their damnation if they refused to worship him? That hardly seemed fair.

I decided to confront him on the subject. Angry, he turned his back, refusing to talk about it and accusing me of always picking on him. That night I saw him for what he was, a jealous, petulant child who always had to get his way. If I refused to play by his rules, he was just going to take his bat and his ball and go home, leaving me standing in an empty field. He only wanted to be with me if I let him be in charge.

We broke up over that. He wouldn't budge, and I just couldn't understand where he was coming from. We agreed to see other people, and I threw out all the things that reminded me of him. Still, it's hard to get over your first love, and I continued to have a weak spot for him. After I left high school, I even went to a college where he was held in great esteem. In fact, he was so admired that we studied his life and work with the same dedication with which we studied the writings of William Shakespeare. Indeed, we gave more attention to God, since after all he had created Shakespeare, and in comparison to God's writings the Bard's tales were the mutterings of an incoherent fool.

Surrounded by other people who had known God for a while, I asked them what kind of relationships they'd had with him. I was sort of impressed by, and maybe even a little bit jealous of, his ability to maintain so many relationships I hadn't even known about. I'd always assumed that he had other friends, but I had no idea just how busy he was when he wasn't with me. I wondered if all of these people meant as much to him as he'd said I did. It was sort of like meeting someone at a party and finding out he not only knew my first boyfriend, but had slept with him once, possibly even while we were still dating. Only in this case, it was lots of people who knew him. Eager for answers about what went wrong between us, I demanded to know if they had the same impressions of him that I did and if he'd treated them the same way he'd treated me.

Some people had dumped God just as I had, tired of his arrogance. Others claimed to still be happily with him, although I frequently saw them sneaking around behind his back. I confess that for a time I also got back together with God. I know, I know, I should have known better. It's the same story they all use. But you see, I ran into him one Sunday at an Episcopal church I was visiting with a friend, and he said he'd changed. And really, it seemed he had. No longer the fire-and-brimstone Baptist God I'd known for most of my life, he was a more refined, almost contemplative God. He liked music and poetry. He spoke softly instead of always yelling. It was a side of him I'd never seen before. He said he understood now that not everyone responded to him in the same way. Sometimes he even kicked back and enjoyed a little wine. Maybe, I thought, we could work out the problems we'd had. After all, we were both a little older, a little wiser. Perhaps all we'd needed was some time apart.

So I agreed to give it another try. But after a few months of harmony, I realized that despite his claims and my hopes, he was the same old God. He might have exchanged his tacky polyester suit for some elegant vestments, and his new place with its soaring cathedral ceilings was definitely an improvement over the shabby gold-carpeted bachelor pad of his past, but underneath it all he still insisted that I put him first in my life. Whenever I tried to do anything without him, he complained. And if I questioned his ways, then he turned into the cold and distant God I remembered. Finally, after one too many arguments about what he needed from the relationship and how I wasn't good enough for him, I gave him up for good.

That was over ten years ago, and I've moved on with my life. There have been other men, other relationships, other breakups. Today I am a totally different person than I was when I was with God. Still, from time to time, especially around the holidays, something will remind me of him, and for a moment I'll think fondly about the good times we had together. Sometimes I even miss him, and I wonder how he's doing or who he's with now. But then I remember his temper, and his refusal to compromise, and I know I made the right decision to leave him. Maybe someday we can be friends again, but for now I think we both need our space.

Besides, I know I can do better.

Naughty or Nice

If my mother was right, I won't be getting any presents from Santa this year. Neither will my friend Deb. After yesterday we're definitely on the Naughty list, and I don't think there's any going back.

I never thought I'd be in this position. I've always been decidedly in the Nice camp. I was one of those kids who never got in trouble at school, never raided the liquor cabinet, never sneaked out of the house in the middle of the night to go joyriding. Even now I only exceed the speed limit when driving the dog to the vet after he's eaten an entire bag of M&M's and needs his stomach pumped again. And Santa has always rewarded me accordingly—except for a few undesired sweaters, socks, and underwear during my late prepubescent years.

But I don't think any of this will save me from a joyless Christmas this time around. I will explain.

Beginning this spring, there has been a war going on at the park where I take my dog, Roger, for his morning swim and romp. It seems that a certain group of pedestrians and joggers decided the dogs were creating a hazard. I won't bore you with the details. Suffice it to say that some stupid people with nothing better to do called the parks department and demanded that the canine menace be thwarted.

The result was that all year the park has been swarming with rangers. Rangers who like nothing better than to present us with tickets—$10 for five minutes of barking, $15 for roaming without a license, $25 for an unleashed dog, $40 for failure to produce a bag for picking up poop. Since some of us break 30 or 40 of the different rules on a daily basis, just taking the dog for a walk requires the use of American Express.

What makes it worse is that some of the rangers seem to take inordinate joy in enforcing the new doggie restrictions. One in particular has been a repeated nuisance, appearing at the most inopportune moments— like when Roger has just emerged from the off-limits pond and is indisputably dripping wet ($50 fine)—and swiftly dispensing her version of justice. This park harpy has been especially cruel to Deb, who one day was forced to run clear through the park while clutching her Brittany spaniel, Gracie, in her arms to avoid a nasty incident involving previous unpaid tickets and impoundment.

Which brings us to the fateful events of yesterday, when Deb and I were having a quiet little lunch at the local sandwich shop. We were just finishing up when who should walk in but this very same devil in far-too-snug blue polyester pants.

"Let's get out of here before she recognizes me," said Deb, who still isn't over the running-away incident.

Holding newspapers over our faces, we escaped through the back door and into the parking lot. That's when we noticed the animal control van sitting nearby. In fact, it was parked right next to Deb's car.

"Let's see if there are any dogs in there we can liberate," said Deb, peering in the windows.

There were no dogs, but as I stared at the van my hatred of all it stood for boiled over. I reached into my pocket and felt there the Swiss Army knife I keep for various harmless purposes. Suddenly, an evil thought leaped unbidden into my heretofore pure mind. I wavered there on the edge between Naughty and Nice. And then I crossed over.

"We could slash the tires," I said, shocked that such words would come out of my mouth.

Deb looked at me. "That would be really awful," she said.

"The worst thing we've ever done," I said, kicking tentatively at the rear wheel.

"Give me the knife," she said.

But it was my idea, so I got to go first. With Deb acting as lookout, I knelt down and gave the van's tire a poke with the blade. It went in, but not enough to do much damage. I pushed harder, and the steel sank into the rubber. My heart filled with joy as I imagined the hateful ranger attempting to do her dirty work, only to find herself stranded with a flat.

"OK," said Deb. "My turn."

I handed her the knife and stood in front of her to screen her from the view of anyone who might happen to pass by. I heard a giggle as Deb did her own dirty work. Then came the "ouch."

"What did you do?" I hissed.

"I cut myself a little," said Deb.

I turned around. Deb had her finger in her mouth.

"It's OK," she said. "It's just a nick."

I looked at the blood on her shirt. And the blood on the knife. And the blood on the ground.

"Take your finger out of your mouth," I said.

Deb pulled her finger out and held it up. The tip slumped to one side like a toppled wedding cake.

"Get in the car," I said.

We managed to sort of stop the bleeding by wrapping Deb's hand in the oh-so-unsanitary towel we use to dry off the dogs after they swim. Then we drove to the hospital.

"Do you realize that between us we are 75 years old and we just slashed the tires of an animal control truck?"

said Deb seriously as we waited at a light.

"I know," I said, still high on the thrill of being Naughty. "Wasn't it great?"

We managed to make it to the hospital, where we encountered a number of different people while en route to getting Deb's finger stitched up. Each one asked how she had cut herself, and each time she and I would look at each other and laugh uncontrollably.

"I think I'll just put down here that you were cutting something and it slipped," said the admitting nurse after asking what happened and then seeing our expressions of barely suppressed glee.

Six hours, seven stitches, and $200 later, we were back in the car.

"Well, I certainly learned something from this little escapade," said Deb seriously as we drove home.

"I'll say," I agreed, wondering if pretending to feel remorse for our felonious actions might still earn us a few small presents from Mr. Claus.

We looked at each other for a moment, and I knew Deb was thinking the same thing. "Next time we need to use a bigger knife," we said in unison.

Santa, are you listening?

An Open Memo to Mattel

To: Mattel New Products Division
From: Mike Ford
Re: Christian Toy Market

As the Christian right continues to breed and grow like mold on a rotting piece of cheese, more and more highly religious children are being let loose upon the world. Like their less pious counterparts, these kids are hungry for fun. Unfortunately, because of their parents' belief that too many modern toys promote violence and ill will, encourage unacceptable variations in traditional sex roles, and foster open-minded attitudes that could result in the demise of church-sanctioned bigotry, most of these youngsters are not afforded the opportunity to enjoy the playthings other children enjoy. While certainly sad for the children thus affected, this situation provides an unexpected benefit for the forward-thinking entrepreneur in the form of an enormous untapped toy market. Ready for positive, Bible-centered toys, Christian parents are ripe for the picking by a marketer with a savvy plan and an enticing product.

To that end, I offer this suggestion for a new line of action figures, to be called Holy Heroes and Heroines or, should a more modern approach be considered appropriate, Bible Buttkickers. Just as Barbie and her friends captured the hearts and imaginations of children the world over, the Bible Buttkickers would find a welcoming audience in today's Christian youngsters who, yearning to experience something of modern life, have been searching for a toy line to call their own.

Central to the line, of course, is the Christ figure, who would come complete with poseable arms and legs and real hair and beard. A G.I. Joe for the Jesus set, he would come with a basic wardrobe of simple robe and removable sandals. Other ensembles would, naturally, be available separately depending upon the play set being utilized. Some of the many possibilities include the Loaves and Fishes wardrobe complete with plastic bread and fish, the Sermon on the Mount festive garment, and the annual Commemorative Collector's Edition Ascension to Heaven ensemble.

The figures are, as you will see, just the beginning of the franchise. The real market will be in the creation of accessories, particularly play sets. As they draw on stories from the both the Old and the New Testament, the range of possible sets and figures to use in them is diverse and potentially unending.

As ideas for initial play sets to launch the line, I propose the following:

The Original Sin Play Set
Craftily melding an important moral lesson with hours of playtime fun, this Garden of Eden set is resplendent with plastic ferns, realistic-looking flowers, and a grand Tree of Life that stretches its branches out to form a canopy. Also central to the scheme is a rubber serpent, which can be wound gracefully about the Tree's branches. Adam and Eve dolls, each covered by strategically placed, nonremovable leaves, can cavort for hours before the beautiful backdrop until, tempted by the serpent, the Eve doll reaches up and takes one of the lifelike apples dangling overhead. When the apple is removed

from the tree, the entire set instantly collapses, leaving the dolls stranded and ashamed. Suddenly embarrassed by their nakedness, they can then opt to cover themselves with any one of the many ensembles available in the Sin Wear line.

The Demon-Possessed Swine Play Set

Based on the story in which Jesus delivers a man from the legion of demons possessing him by casting the evil spirits into a herd of unfortunate pigs, this set comes complete with a foot-high plastic cliff and seven plastic porkers. When a switch is turned on (batteries not included), the cliff begins to vibrate, sending the little plastic pigs scuttling across its top until they tumble off the edge. A microchip in the cliff emits lifelike squealing and screaming sounds as the demon-possessed swine fall to their doom. The Possessed Man figure sports an ingeniously designed head with a face on either side. One face is maddened, the other calm. When a button on the doll's back is pressed, the head turns to present the desired possessed or nonpossessed face, with the other face hidden by the doll's long hair.

Jonah and the Whale Play Set

Appropriate for bath-time fun or use in the pool, the key selling point of this set is a large rubber whale, into whose mouth the Jonah figure fits neatly. Children will experience hours of joy making the whale splash through the water as they pretend to take Jonah to Nineveh. When squeezed, the whale spews the Jonah doll, appropriately covered in slimelike glaze, from its throat. Additional packages of slime, in various colors, may be purchased separately. Production Note: The whale figure should not be large enough to swallow an actual infant or small pet, as initial testing has found the temptation is often too strong to resist. Of a similar bent is the Noah and the Ark Play Set, which consists of a boat and various sets of animals. The ark holds only a limited number of figures, and those that don't fit may be drowned accordingly by the child, for whom the term "playing God" will take on an entirely new meaning.

The Jezebel Play Set

For children blessed with more lenient parents, this amusing set features a lovely simulated stone bath that can actually be filled with water and made to bubble by means of an ingenuous pump hidden underneath. The striking Jezebel doll (also sold separately) has fully washable hair and a larger bosom than the other female dolls. She can recline in the rolling waters of the tub until such time as she spies any of the male figures and attempts to seduce them by blinking her lifelike lashes and pursing her lips. A lesson is learned when the Jezebel doll is later pushed from a window and devoured by dogs for her wicked ways. Because the doll is completely edible and coated with a light beef flavoring, real dogs may be incorporated into the play experience, making the whole thing utterly thrilling for everyone as the nontoxic figure is torn to bits and the moral is driven home.

The Samson and Delilah Play Set

Drawing on the enormous popularity of the Cut-N-Curl Barbie head, this set utilizes realistic hair on the Samson doll. Using ordinary household shears, the child can render the Samson doll bald. Also appealing are his pop-out eyes, ejected from the head by squeezing the sides forcefully. By pushing a button on the doll's back, children can activate the Mighty Muscle Action function and cause the newly blinded Samson doll to push apart the collapsible pillars of the Philistine temple set, bringing it crashing down on any dolls in the area. Replacement hair may be sold in packs of six.

The Jael Play Set

This set will appeal to the many parents searching for strong women role models. Recreating the story of Jael, the brave heroine who saved the Jews from destruction by killing an enemy general, this set comes with a basic tent and General figure. The Jael doll comes with her own plastic hammer and tent peg. When hammered into the cunningly designed skull of the sleeping General, the peg causes realistic-looking blood (edible and nontoxic) to flow from a refillable cavity in the doll's head, making this set ideal for repeated play. Note: No mention should be made on accompanying literature of the fact that Jael first seduced the General and then killed him in his post-coital slumber, as this would create confusion regarding the whole virginity issue.

The Persecution of the Christians Play Set

Composed of a large arena, this play set comes with 12 fish-scented action figures. On either end of the set are doors that can be opened. After the selected dolls are put into the arena, ordinary house cats may be pushed through the doors and into the ring. Drawn to the scent of the fish, the cats will tear apart the dolls, which are completely edible, thus giving the children a fleeting glimpse of what it might have been like to be Christians during the time of Jesus. Players may, if they wish, bet on which dolls will last the longest by using the realistic plastic coins provided. Additional figures in liver, chicken, and beef scents are available in packages of ten.

Plagues of Egypt Play Set

This action-packed set recreates the deadly plagues visited on the Egyptians when Pharaoh reneged on his promise to let the Israelites go free. It comes equipped with rubber locusts, a horde of plastic frogs, and water that turns to blood when exposed to air. Most exciting of all is the Angel of Death figure, which swoops over the set and causes the oldest male dolls to cease working unless their homes have been marked with the powdered blood provided. Included with each set is a Moses doll, which, when a string is pulled, repeats the phrase "I told you so" over and over again in a mocking tone.

The Tower of Babel Play Set

Less an actual play set than a game of strategy, this set is made up of hundreds of plastic bricks. Players take turns adding bricks to the tower, building it to greater and greater heights. Each player selects an action figure and places her or his figure on the top of the tower after each successive turn. If the tower falls, that figure is considered deceased, and the game begins again with the remaining players. When only one player remains, the others get to stone his figure to death for the sin of pride, using the leftover bricks.

The Ark of the Covenant Play Set

A favorite of adventurous children who enjoy outdoor activities, this realistic Ark can be buried in a sandbox or in a yard. The objective of the game is to then find and dig up this replica of the most important Biblical artifact. Before opening it, players must memorize an elaborate ritual outlined in the game book provided. If opened incorrectly, the Ark emits a powerful but ultimately harmless electric shock.

The Birth of Jesus Play Set

The first in the Life of Christ series of sets, this is more than just your average Nativity. Based on a stable motif, the set contains numerous livestock and realistic plastic hay, which can be placed in the adorable manger. It also comes with both a Mary and a Joseph doll. Although outwardly sexless, the Mary doll does have a hole in her back. When mixed with water and poured into the hole, the Holy Spirit powder provided will cause the doll to swell as though pregnant, and a cleverly concealed Baby Jesus will emerge when the Mary doll is squeezed. It can then be wrapped in swaddling clothes and adored by all.

The Crucifixion Play Set

Sure to be one of the more popular modules in the series, this set comes complete with three plastic crosses made to scale. Easily set up in a sandbox or other appropriately dry location, the crosses contain holes for cleverly designed nails, which are also included. The set requires the additional purchase of the Hanging Jesus, whose hands and feet are already pierced for easy play. Two thief figures come with the set. Other figures may be dressed to portray Roman guards, grieving apostles, the crowd, etc. This may also be piggybacked with a Last Supper Play Set featuring some form of oven fueled by a 75-watt light bulb for the baking of bread.

The Resurrection Play Set

A natural follow-up to the previous set, this one comes with a fully-realized tomb and large plastic stone to cover the entrance. After removing Hanging Jesus from the cross, children may then wrap him in the burial cloth provided and place him on a slab inside the tomb. By moving a lever, the slab is turned over, revealing a Resurrected Jesus figure (included). The set also comes with a Shroud of Turin, which, when exposed to light, reveals the face of the Lord on its surface.

The End Times Play Set

The most ambitious of the sets, this apocalyptic wonder recreates the horrors of the End Times in graphic detail, complete with fire-and-brimstone backdrop. Created especially for this ensemble are the frightening

Seven-Headed Beast and the Whore of Babylon figure. When switched on, the Beast walks menacingly across the play set with the Whore astride its back, leveling the world and trampling those figures that steadfastly refuse to receive the Mark of the Beast (ink pad and 666 stamp included).

As you can see from the above examples, the Bible Buttkickers line has the potential to become one of the best-selling toy lines of all time. I suggest the immediate creation of prototypes and the beginning of product testing with Sunday School children across the country.

In addition to these play sets, many new and exciting related accessories can be created, allowing children to dress up as their favorite biblical characters for hours of fun. Some of the many possible items to be manufactured include the Bible Belt, the Walking on Water Wings, the Holy Rollers Hair Styler, the Do-It-Yourself Saint Kit, and the plastic First Stone for casting at one's enemies.

Gone to the Dogs

Before I got Roger, my black Lab, my life was like that of most people without dogs. My daily routine was orderly and generally uneventful. I did errands, went to the Laundromat, and ordered Chinese food without a second thought. I was content with an existence that, if not precisely thrilling, was at least reassuring in its regularity. I knew what to expect when I left the house and went out into the world.

But not anymore. Now my life is filled with intrigue, and a simple walk into town to go to the post office has about it the air of a secret mission, with danger behind every tree and both friends and enemies waiting around every corner. Since Roger has become part of my life, I have become a player in a game I didn't even know existed, one that was begun centuries ago and will likely go on for centuries to come.

I am speaking, of course, about the war between those who are dog people and those who aren't. It is a fiercely fought struggle, and the playing field consists of city streets, public buildings, newly seeded lawns, and anywhere else the two factions might encounter one another. It is a world filled with strange alliances, bitter feuds, and fated loves, where deals are closed with the subtle shake of a tail, and a single snarl or lift of the leg can signal the start of a new skirmish.

Before getting into the details of the actual battle, we

must look first at the players at the center of it all—the dogs. There are two classes of dogs: Snooty, ill-mannered ones and good-natured, friendly ones. In the first category are what I have come to call Football Dogs, named for the almost uncontrollable urge they elicit in people they meet to drop-kick them several blocks. Frequently seen riding primly in shopping baskets or mincing fussily along at the ends of bejeweled leashes, Football Dogs include but are not limited to shih tzus, Lhasa apsos, miniature poodles, and basically anything that appears in public sporting a bow.

The second category is known commonly as Dawgs. The blue-collar citizens of the canine world, this group consists of any dog that could be found sleeping outside a gas station and is composed primarily of larger breeds such as retrievers, rottweilers, shepherds, and mongrels. Whereas Football Dogs tend to sit in the backseats of cars, trying to keep their fur in place, Dawgs are almost always seen hanging perilously far out of open windows, preferably truck windows, while attempting to inhale the whole of the great outdoors.

This system of classifying dogs, while strict, is not without its leniencies. Not all small dogs are of the Football variety. Pugs, for instance, are included in the Dawg family, mainly because they are wonderfully ugly and don't give a damn. And some large dogs, such as the more excessive breeds of collies, border on Football territory when they exhibit un-Dawglike characteristics. Then there are dogs, such as shar-peis and chows, that inhabit their own world, set apart by their exotic origins. Silent and aloof, they remain mysteries even to their owners, who generally regret that they did not purchase terriers or beagles instead.

The foot soldiers in the war between the pro-dog and con-dog camps are, of course, the humans. Depending on where one lives, these people take various forms. Because I live near a large public park, I am most familiar with that particular venue and the types of people who frequent it. At the park where Roger and I go, the two armies can be clearly divided into the categories of Activity People and Dog People. In general, the two groups despise one another wholeheartedly. Each thinks the other is selfish, undisciplined, and just plain stupid. Whenever possible, we remind one another of these facts in loud voices.

Like the different categories of dogs, each category of person has its own unique qualities that set it apart. This deserves some exploration. Because I am nothing if not fair, I will attend to the antidog group first. Activity People come in various forms, the most common ones being Walkers and Joggers, Fishermen, Bread Throwers, and Picnickers.

Fishermen are a problem for only part of the year, although what they lack in frequency of appearance they more than make up for in surliness. They do not like dogs because they are convinced that jumping into the water and swimming after sticks somehow frightens off the fish. They see the pond as their domain and dogs as invading marauders intent on pillaging and general destruction. Their favorite weapons are fishing poles, which they wave menacingly while shouting obscenities. Fortunately, they generally wear very heavy rubber boots and seldom are able to actually carry out their threats to chase you out of the park. Also, they tend to be relatively slow thinkers, making verbal battles a surreal and satisfying experience. My favorite insult ever hurled by a Fisherman was, "I hope your dog takes a crap on somebody's lawn." The dog owner's winning retort: "I'm sure he will, and I bet it will be yours."

Bread Throwers and Picnickers are, as a whole, a more moderate group, although if one has a little time and is willing to put forth the effort, they can be pushed beyond their limits, resulting in some fascinating displays of anger. Bread Throwers are almost always elderly women or parents with children and are easily spotted by the large plastic bags of stale bread they carry with them everywhere they go. Dogs frustrate this group due to their tendency to either eat the bread scattered around for the birds or to chase and/or eat the birds themselves. When confronted by dogs, the Bread Throwers can be expected to look at you with surprised expressions and, if especially timid, break into violent weeping while telling any surrounding small children how bad you and your dog are. Picnickers are slightly more volatile, since what the dogs steal from them is not so much old bread as it is nicely roasted beef or other things they meant to eat themselves. I once saw a group of seven dogs stampede through a picnic, resulting in a merry chase and muzzles coated with coleslaw.

Walkers and Joggers are most definitely the worst of the lot. These hardy souls seem to think it is great fun to traipse all over the park from morning to night, and they most definitely do not like dogs. Dogs, of course, are very fond of people running, as they think it is their duty to chase them and bring them down. While this can be amusing to watch, anyone who has been a member of this group for more than a month or two has learned to carry Mace or pepper spray, which is not so much fun for the dogs as you might think. Some of the more foolish ones, who clearly have not been at it for long, run with sticks, which any dog owner will tell you is the finest way of assuring that every dog within a ten-mile radius will show up for the chase.

Despite their myriad dangers, Walkers and Joggers are the favorite prey of dogs, since they are about as numerous as gazelle on an African plain. They also tend toward the physical in their attacks, which for a dog with any sense of adventure is merely an invitation to try harder. Whereas a Bread Thrower will simply threaten to call a ranger and tell on you, a Jogger will run faster and flail his arms, causing any pursuing dogs to become maddened with excitement. Joggers can also be counted on to provide excellent opportunities for verbal sparring. Last summer a woman who jogs daily past our morning dog group at the park turned and called angrily, "Those dogs should be on leashes." Without missing a beat, my friend James retorted with an answer I dearly wish I could claim as my own. Fixing the woman with a withering look, he snarled, "You should run faster."

Which brings us to the other side—the Dog People. These come in various guises as well, and may be subcategorized into Leashers, Permissives, and Antiauthoritarians. The least threatening to Activity People are the Leashers, who almost universally obey the informative signs at parks reminding everyone that dogs belong on leads. Generally bankers, lawyers, and Sunday School teachers, they are the nerds of the Dog People, and their dogs are appropriately boring, generally nervous purebred spaniels with unsuitable names like Montgomery and Elizabeth. The Leashers are tolerated by the other dog people, but only because anyone who brings a dog to the park can't be entirely bad. They are not, however, considered loyal soldiers in the war, and they are kept in the dark about the more clandestine activities of the group, such as ALL DOGS MUST BE ON LEASHES sign stealing, the slashing of animal control truck tires, and owner-encouraged squirrel chasing.

Smack in the middle of the pack—temperament-wise—are the Permissives. A Permissive is generally female and in all likelihood also has several cats (rescued from shelters) and a bumper sticker on her 1986 Volvo wagon saying practice RANDOM ACTS OF KINDNESS. A Permissive's dog is usually some kind of mutt, preferably one rescued from a horrible fate and that still bears scars from the ordeal, such as a missing leg, torn ear, or bullet wound. The Permissive believes in giving her dog some freedom to run with the pack, but is also mindful of the needs of others, including Activity People. When her dog runs near a picnic, she firmly calls him back and often apologizes to the startled diners. In her more daring moments, she will ignore the warnings to keep her dog leashed at all times, but she is ever watchful for signs of rangers or other authority figures and will quickly call her dog to her side should the threat of danger arise.

Antiauthoritarians just don't give a crap. The lone wolves of the pro-dog faction, they believe that parks are for dogs, not people, and that anyone who disagrees with them is an asshole. Antiauthoritarians keep their dogs on leashes only until they are safely away from traffic. Within park grounds they set them free to do as they wish. Their dogs drink from public water fountains, pee wantonly on the most endangered of trees, and roam freely on walking paths. Antiauthoritarians loathe Activity People and will pretend not to notice if their dogs surround and maul one. They favor either very large or very lively dogs and are especially fond of breeds possessing both qualities. Their dogs are named things like Louie, Carver, and McKinley, and they come equipped with all kinds of dog toys, ranging from simple tennis balls to elaborate rope-and-rubber-toy contraptions designed for hours of fun. Antiauthoritarians and their dogs are in the park by dawn and sometimes stay until well after dark, even in winter.

As can be imagined, the fiercest fights occur when an Antiauthoritarian encounters an aggressive Activity Person. Generally battles happen when a dog does something like steal a child's ice-cream cone or knock over a jogger and the owner is caught laughing heartily. The Activity Person will then begin to bellow accusations of impropriety, causing the Antiauthoritarian to respond with unkind comments about the offended person's mother, sister, and maiden aunt. Unless one backs down, things will progress to more heated exchanges, sometimes resulting in physical violence. More often, however, the encounter ends with both parties screaming "Fuck you!" as often as possible while walking in opposite directions. The dog, of course, has long forgotten all about it and is busy doing something else.

I confess that I am squarely in the Antiauthoritarian camp. It seems to me that people have a lot more places to go than do dogs and that dogs should be allowed to enjoy what small territory they can stake out. I love to see Roger take a flying leap into the pond next to a Fisherman, and the look of fear on Joggers' faces when they see him coming at full speed down a hill is pure delight. Oblivious to the people around him, Roger romps through life with a carefree attitude. "I'm in your way?" he seems to say to the Activity People shooting him dirty looks as he runs by, ears flapping. "Bite me!"

This does not always win us a lot of friends. Not everyone enjoys being greeted by a muddy, 110-pound Labrador fresh from a swim in the pond. But we don't care. We recklessly bound our way through the park looking for fun, and woe unto those who cross us. One sunny afternoon, as we were enjoying a hearty game of stick, a red-faced woman accosted us. "Excuse me," she said harshly, "but can't you read the signs? Dogs have to be on leashes. What if your dog attacks my little girl?"

I looked at the little girl, who was happily trying to pull Roger's ears while he licked her face. "I'll tell you what," I said politely to the woman. "If he bites her, you can have him shot. And if your little girl bites him, I'll have her shot."

The woman snatched up her child and ran, leaving us free to enjoy the rest of our game. In the battle of the dogs and the people, the dogs are way ahead, at least in our park.

Could You Hurry Up? I'm Starting to Cramp

I should have known I would have trouble with sex the day Missy Graham took me back to her house after our fourth-grade class let out for the day and showed me her father's stack of *Playboys*. As we sat on the bed in Missy's room, sucking on lemons sprinkled with salt and looking at Miss November's auburn-colored snatch, all I could think about was that it reminded me of one of the Tribbles from that famous *Star Trek* episode. I imagined Captain Kirk trying to stuff it back inside Miss November before it took over the ship, and I giggled. It was not an auspicious beginning.

I was lucky in one respect—I came of age during the 1970s, and like most kids of that era, I was introduced to sex by Judy Blume. Because I read so much, I knew her books inside and out. And even if I hadn't, our favorite school activity was to sit in the back of the library and read the dirty parts of all the Blume novels to one another.

While *Are You There God? It's Me, Margaret* was the most well-known Blume book, it was for girls, and its depictions of breast development and periods was not especially interesting to me. Her book for boys, *Then Again, Maybe I Won't*, talked about masturbation, and that was a little more exciting. I still remember reading the book while on a picnic with my mother. As she sat in the sun, munching away on her peanut butter sandwich, I read the book as quickly as possible, terrified that she would ask to see it and take it away from me.

While these books were intriguing, I was more fascinated by Blume's later book *Forever*. This had actual sex in it, and because of that was kept on the special reserve shelf in our library, requiring a parent's permission to check it out. But one of my friends, whose parents were very freethinking, had bought her her very own copy, and she kindly shared it with the rest of us. We sat, spellbound, as Sheila read us the most lurid parts of the book in her best dramatic voice. When the two main characters in the novel finally tried to have sex, we waited breathlessly as Blume, through Sheila, described it for us.

But even this was nothing compared to the scandalous *Endless Love*. None of my friends were old enough to actually see the Brooke Shields movie, but we did manage to get hold of a copy of the book version, and with it we hit pay dirt. It came in the form of anal sex. As I recall, the Brooke Shields character and her boyfriend decide to try it in the back door, and there is quite a good description of it.

We read this passage again and again to one another, beside ourselves with the sordidness of it all. We couldn't imagine anyone sticking anything up a butt except a thermometer. Certainly no boy would want his nice clean willy near one. It was all too much. I couldn't believe that there was really anyone who enjoyed that kind of thing. Surely I myself never would. It was unthinkable.

But then, a few years later, I discovered a *Playgirl* hidden beneath my cousin Sherri's bed. I was in her room, innocently listening to records, and found it when I went looking for the sleeve to the Barry Manilow album I was playing. I pulled the magazine out and flipped through it, staring at all of the naked men standing there with their you-know-whats hanging out for the world to see. Unlike Miss November's muff, these didn't make me giggle.

And then there was John Pellico Jr. I may have misspelled his name slightly, but I recall vividly what he looked like. Dark-haired and mustached, he was wearing a red flannel shirt, open to reveal the hair on his chest. And then there was his impressive...thingy. As I stared at it hanging between his hairy thighs, suddenly that passage in *Endless Love* didn't quite seem so ridiculous after all.

It was a turning point. After that I was determined to find out all about sex and what people did with one another. The only problem was that I was too shy to actually ask anyone. So I had to find out in other ways, which meant looking for answers in books.

My parents had lots of books, so I started there. After some searching, I came across a battered copy of *The Christian Couple's Guide to Intimacy* found behind some religious titles in my mother's bookcase. It was a rather graphic book, complete with line drawings and diagrams, and it was extremely explicit about exactly how the act of intercourse should be undertaken. I read it over and over again, memorizing the details of what the author described as the perfect wedding night. This entailed the groom lying at his wife's side while he stroked first her nipples and then her labia. When she was ready to proceed, and she was supposed to tell him when the time came, he was to enter her gently. Then—and this is the most baffling part—he was supposed to pause in mid entry for several minutes while he regained his composure, lest he ejaculate from the excitement and ruin things completely.

At the time that I read this, I assumed that the act of Christian intercourse must be the most exciting thing to ever happen to a man. It would not be the only thing about organized religion I would later find to be highly overrated.

Apart from the step-by-step instructions, the part of the book I remember most vividly is a drawing of the female genitalia, drawn from the perspective of the artist staring directly into the slightly parted lips of some model's Georgia O'Keefe. Everything was neatly labeled, with arrows pointing to the various parts. It reminded me a bit of the diagram in my history textbook outlining the events at the Battle of Bull Run, only instead of arrows indicating troop movements and Confederate defense strategies, there were lines leading to the clitoris and the labia majora.

While most of it was pretty self-explanatory, I was very confused by the notion that there were two openings in the genitalia, one for urination and one for—presumably—the penis to enter during sex. I returned to the book over and over, trying very hard to remember which hole was which. While I was beginning to suspect that I would never find myself needing to use such knowledge, I very much wanted to make sure I knew which hole to concentrate on should I ever be required to do so. Little did I know that I should have been paying more attention to the drawing of the rectum on page 73.

The cumulative effect of the book, the diagrams, and my own vivid imagination was that the idea of heterosexual relations was not one I cared to dwell on for long. And since there were no discussions of what two men could do together on *their* wedding night, I was forced to make up my own scenarios.

In general, these involved the men from *Adam 12* rescuing me from a robbery attempt. From time to time I would cast John Pellico Jr. as the robber, and then I was always torn between being saved or remaining captive for an indefinite period while John tried to extract an exorbitant ransom and my parents haggled over the price.

Other than that, I wasn't sure what we would all do together. I think I had some vague notion that it would involve having a cookout and maybe playing some badminton, but the details were sketchy.

I have friends who tell me wild stories about all of the sex they had as adolescents with other neighborhood boys, friends at summer camp, and even various distant relations during family reunions. Apparently these men lived in very different neighborhoods from mine. Apart from one awkward sleepover when my friend Steve pretended to roll over and accidentally put his hand on my dick, nothing of interest happened to me.

High school and college were no better. In fact, during college I somehow found myself dating a headstrong Italian girl named Michelle. I don't know how it happened exactly. All I remember is that one day we were sharing a biology class and the next she was making out with me in the little room we used to store frozen cat corpses for anatomy class. We remained boyfriend and girlfriend for the better part of my sophomore year, and the only reason I was spared actually having to sleep with her was that she felt very strongly about our Christian college's edict against engaging in sexual intercourse. While the idea of sex with Michelle was not entirely unpleasant, I was glad to be spared the encounter, primarily because I had long forgotten the diagram from my mother's book showing which hole was which and feared making a mistake.

Thus I entered adulthood still wildly unprepared for what was to come. As a result, on the night that I decided it was time to dive headfirst into the world of gay sex, I had no idea what I was in for. But I had an apartment, I had the will, and I was in the heart of gay New York. I headed out that June night ready for action.

I found it at the only bar I knew of. After standing around for an hour and trying to figure out just how it was all done, I was relieved when a man approached me and started talking to me. His pickup line was, "What's your favorite movie?"

Deciding that this was a trick question, and being too flustered to actually think of a movie I'd seen recently, I blurted out, "*Escape from Witch Mountain.* How about you?"

Either I caught him off-guard or he was too horny to care about my apparent Disney obsession. Whatever the reason, he smiled and told me that his personal favorite was *The Philadelphia Story.* Not having seen that movie, I nodded vaguely in agreement. This seemed to be enough for him, and a few minutes later he asked me home.

We went to my place because it was closest. Once inside, it all went very quickly, and before I knew it I was in bed with a naked man for the very first time in my life. Trying to remember everything I could from *The Christian Couple's Guide to Intimacy,* I went through the wedding night steps in order, simply switching the pronouns from "she" to "he" and the word "bride" to "trick." It worked perfectly well at first. I managed to get through the kissing, the breast fondling, and the stroking with ease. I even threw in a few things the author of the *Guide* had failed to include, proud of myself for being so bold my first time out.

Then I got to the intercourse part, and suddenly things got dicey. Even though I couldn't recall the exact layout of the vagina diagram, I knew roughly how a woman worked. But even though I'd imagined anal sex with a man, I hadn't been confronted with the actual plumbing or the physical details of how it was done. There I was, lying on my partner's left side, stroking him. His moaning made it clear to me that he was ready to proceed. But I didn't know where to go from there.

"Are you a top or a bottom?" he asked, sensing a pause in the action.

I looked at him blankly. I had no idea what he meant. As far as I knew, tops and bottoms were fashion terms or directional signals printed on refrigerator cartons. No one had ever asked me this before. Once again I tried a neutral approach.

"What do you want me to be?" I asked, hoping that putting the ball in his court would give me a tactical advantage.

"Fuck me," he answered breathlessly.

I couldn't imagine many Christian women saying that to their Christian husbands on their honeymoon nights, but I got the message loud and clear. Now that the whole top and bottom thing was sorted out, we could continue. Only I couldn't tell this man that he was my first time, that I had zero experience in the fucking department.

Once again helping me out, he reached over and took a condom from the bedside table. I'd had enough sense to put some out before I left the house, having seen enough safer sex materials to know they might come in handy at some point. I watched as he opened it deftly with his teeth, removed the rubber, and slid it over my dick. Then he pulled his knees back and looked at me expectantly.

"Got any lube?" he asked.

Lube. I hadn't thought about lube. I didn't know I might need it. I'd assumed the condoms came ready to use. But apparently this was one more thing I'd gotten confused about.

"I'll be right back," I said, as if somewhere in the apartment there was a whole vat of lube I'd simply forgotten to wheel out and place beside the bed.

I ran into the bathroom and threw open the medicine cabinet. The only thing in there was a tube of Crest. It might leave everything minty fresh, but I had my doubts about its lubricating qualities. I paused briefly at the Vicks, noting its resemblance to Vaseline, but I remembered from childhood experience that it really didn't feel very nice on the skin.

Finding nothing in the bathroom, I tried the kitchen, frantically looking for olive oil, butter, or even a can of cooking spray. But there was nothing that might be useful. I could hear my beau in the bedroom, calling me back, and I knew I had to find something soon or risk having my debut fuck turn into a complete disaster.

Finally I looked at the sink and saw the dispenser of Yardley's of London Lavender Hand Wash that someone had given me for Christmas months earlier. I'd never used it, finding the scent a little bit cloying, but now it shone before me like the Holy Grail at the end of a long and dangerous journey. Snatching it up triumphantly, I raced back to the bedroom.

My intended was still on his back on the bed, legs spread and eyes willing. Kneeling confidently on the bed, I flipped open the Yardley's and squeezed some onto my hand. By that point I'd figured out what needed lubricating, and I diligently set about making sure everything that needed to be good and slippery was in fact good and slippery.

"That smells great," my soon-to-be first time said.

"Um, yeah," I responded. "It's new. I think it's organic or something."

The hand wash did indeed do the trick. A moment later, I was in like a thief through a wide-open window. Remembering what the book had said, I paused a moment to prevent an abrupt ending to the experience, and then continued on. Like a Labrador discovering water for the first time, I found that everything came quite naturally, and I was both thrilled and relieved to finally be finding out what the big fuss was all about.

And then the bubbles started. They began as foam, really, but as the friction continued they grew in size. A few minutes later, tiny bubbles began to detach from my paramour's sudsy nether parts and float into the room. I stared in horror as they drifted through the air and settled gently on his stomach.

"Hey, what's that?" he asked, his steady stream of grunts and groans interrupted as he poked at the bubble on his chest hair.

I thought maybe he'd ignore the bubble if I thrust a little harder, so I tried that. Unfortunately, the additional effort merely increased the size and frequency of the bubbles, and it wasn't long before his backside had turned into a veritable bubble machine, filling the air with a cascade of shimmery orbs. They landed and popped on our skin, covering us with their lavender scent.

My foray into the wonderful world of homosex had turned into *The Lawrence Welk Show*. I imagined my grandmother sitting on the couch, watching us rut as smiling dancers twirled around the bed and she clapped along merrily. It was all too much to take. I continued with the production for a while longer, but in the end I had to give up before the finale.

You would think that after that I would have given up on sex altogether. But it was only the beginning. As hard as I tried, I couldn't resist the call of the wild forever, and eventually I found myself once more on the search for fun and adventure.

One of the problems with gay sex is that we have very bad role models in the form of gay porn movies and gay porn fiction. From watching such movies or reading such books, it's easy to get the impression that sex between men is always incredibly hot, incredibly clean, and incredibly fulfilling.

The truth is almost always the complete opposite. More often than not, sex with men involves a lot of fumbling with the button flies of 501s, trying to figure out which way the condom rolls, and enduring prolonged coughing fits when stray hairs slide down our throats. It is seldom the smooth operation pornographers would have us believe it is.

Take, for example, the issue of big dicks. I confess that I have something of a fondness for them, and for some time I fantasized about finding a man who had one that would defy description. Well, you should always be careful what you wish for. My fantasy materialized one evening in the form of a very tall, very large, very handsome German man. When he undid his jeans and I saw what lay beneath, I had to be revived by a splash of cold water to the face.

But alas, Gunther had one small problem. Or rather, one very large problem. For while his dick was indeed of Teutonic proportions, getting it filled to capacity with the blood necessary to make it hard meant that other areas of his body had to do without. Unfortunately the result of an erection was that his brain was unable to function fully, making sex with him about as exciting as the *Doctor Who* reruns he insisted on watching during lovemaking.

And when he was erect, there was the tiny matter of what to do with something so large. While it was kind of fun to play with him, it was a little like swinging a Wiffle bat around. Getting my mouth around the whole thing would have required installing hinges, and just the thought of him trying to put it anywhere else made me feel faint. While I tried valiantly to make the most of his natural gifts, in the end I had to abandon Gunther to someone with more relaxed throat muscles and no fear of a future marred by the inconvenience of incontinence.

Then there's the whole problem of expectations. Again, pornographers would have us believe that every sexual encounter is a roller-coaster ride of earthshaking moments of pure ecstasy from beginning to end. But it doesn't work that way. While I would truly like to believe that there are men who spend each moment of their escapades in bed shouting out things like "Oh, yeah, do me harder, you big stud" and "Just like that, baby. Do it. Do it. Do it," I think the reality is somewhat different for most of us.

I, for example, am more likely to be thinking about the fact that I am missing the second half of the miniseries that began the previous night or worrying that perhaps having Indian food for dinner was not as good an idea as it had seemed a few hours before. Rather than staying in the moment and contemplating my partner's handsome face or our impending orgasms, I tend to wander in and out. One second I'll be wondering what I might get my friend Katherine for her upcoming birthday and the next I'll be noticing that the walls need painting again. I may throw in a few halfhearted groans from time to time, but rarely can I bring myself to actually say something along the lines of "Take that big dick" or "Give it to me harder." Even when the action is, in fact, hot and heavy, things are not nearly as thrilling as they are in the fictional word. While one or the other of us does his best to bring things to a boil, I can generally be counted on to be thinking, *Could you hurry up? I'm starting to cramp.*

Maybe it's the fault of *The Christian Couple's Guide to Intimacy.* Maybe I should blame it on watching too many Falcon video releases. Maybe somewhere out there are men who have amazing sex all the time, and they're just keeping it a secret from the rest of us. All I know is that somewhere along the line I got sold a bill of goods, and no one has delivered on it yet. When I lie in bed after another go at launching my own sexual revolution, I feel less like a sated stud from a Gordon Merrick novel and more like the protagonist from *Forever,* who, after her first attempt at sex with her boyfriend ends with his pre-

mature ejaculation, lies on the Oriental carpet in her bedroom listening to her overeager lover washing up in the
bathroom and wonders if it ever gets any better. I hate to
break it to her, but it doesn't.

No Way Out

A couple of weeks ago, I called my mother to talk about Baptists. I'm working on a book of interviews with leaders from various religious traditions, and I needed her input. My mother is a good person to ask about such things because she is Queen of All Baptists. She knows who all the big names are, and all the ins and outs of the doctrinal debates. She should. After years of being a Sunday School teacher, Vacation Bible School leader, and Good News Club instructor (something like a den mother for very pious Cub Scouts), she's now married to a former Baptist minister. It's her dream come true. If she can't be the real thing, she can at least be close to it. It's the principle that's driven every first lady since Martha Washington. Since my own dream is to be married to a porn star, I can relate to her sense of accomplishment.

So, needing ecclesiastical advice, I called her to find out who she thought I should interview for my book to represent the Baptists. The obvious choice was the Rev. Billy Graham, the Elvis of the Bible-thumping set. But I'd already requested an interview with him and been turned down. The publicist who called me said it was because of Reverend Graham's health, but I saw him doing a television interview a few days later, so I knew the real reason lay elsewhere. And I had a good idea where that was. I suspected that someone in the Billy Graham organization had looked up my other books, seen the word "gay," and decided that I wasn't to be trusted. They probably thought I'd ask Reverend Graham about those nasty gerbil stories that have plagued him since his days in the seminary.

My mother, as expected, suggested Graham right off the bat. "He's such a nice man," she said. "I'm sure he'd love to talk to you."

"He said no, Mom," I told her, hoping she'd move on without a fight. "Can you think of anyone else?"

Never one to let a topic die easily, she persisted. "Why did he say no?" she asked. "I'm sure if you asked nicely he'd do it. Did he say why he wouldn't do it?"

We had come to a moment I'd been trying to avoid for years. You see, my mother and I never mention the *G* word. Not *God,* although that one is risky as well. *Gay.* She knows who and what I am. She knows what I write about. But we never, ever talk about it. In general, my family has a policy of never discussing our lives in any greater detail than recounting what our various pets have done recently. It's just better that way. Besides, it had really never come up. When you stick to talking about dogs, things seldom get more complicated than feeding schedules, veterinary procedures, and how to remove vomit stains from silk.

But now we'd moved into new territory, and I decided enough was enough. After two decades of "don't ask, don't tell," it was time to officially come out once and for all.

"He won't do it because I'm gay," I said flatly.

There was a long pause. I could hear her breathing on the other end, as if she'd just run the 500 meters at the Olympics and was exhausted from the effort. She continued to breathe for two or three minutes, just enough for me to wonder if maybe I should call the paramedics. I was looking up her address when she finally spoke.

"You know," she said, "I don't understand why every-

one blames people with AIDS just because they're gay. I
don't see why it matters how someone got it, and I'm sick
and tired of Jimmy Swaggart saying all of those mean
things about gay people. In fact, I wrote him a letter this
morning telling him he isn't very Christian."

Now it was my turn to be speechless. Never mind that
she'd gotten the whole gay people and AIDS thing all
mixed up. She was missing the entire point of what I'd
just told her.

"Did you know Ryan White?" she asked me before I
could think of what to say next.

"Um, no," I said, caught off-guard. "I spoke to his
mother when I was writing my book about AIDS,
though."

"He was a nice boy, and people were very mean to
him," she continued. "That's wrong."

"Ryan wasn't gay, Mom," I said, trying to turn the
conversation back to me. "He was a hemophiliac. And
not all gay people have AIDS."

"I know that," she said in the same tone five-year-olds
use when you've said something really dumb. "I'm just
saying."

After that there was another awkward silence. Then I
told her about something funny the dog had just done,
and she countered with a story about how her two dogs
had done something even more hysterical about two days
ago. We were back on familiar ground, and neither one
of us brought up the gay thing again.

This is the pattern of my life. Every June, when pride
rolls around again, I think about my family and about
the coming-out question. It seems odd to me that I've
never actually sat down with any of them and had The
Talk. Here I am, writing books and essays all about my
gay life for the gay community, yet in my own family the
subject has little or no meaning. Don't get me wrong—
I'm not upset because I feel there's something about me

they don't know. I'm pissed off that I don't have a good coming-out story to share at parties.

I have friends with incredibly dramatic coming-out stories, and I never tire of hearing them. Some told their parents and were immediately sent to Catholic school, therapists, or both. A few were inadvertently caught in the act of discovering their budding sexuality with their Little League coaches or best friends from high school. Still others waited until they just couldn't come up with any more excuses for not being married, and blurted out the true reason over the Passover seder or Thanksgiving dinner. While some have horror stories, most say coming out was a wonderful, liberating experience for them. Very few have neutral feelings about it, and even those with negative experiences enjoy telling the stories like veterans of foreign wars reliving the glorious moments of past battles.

I have no such luck. As hard as I try, I can't imagine any of these scenarios playing themselves out in my family. We don't ask each other personal questions, and Thanksgiving dinner is reserved for discussions of the relative merits of the floats in the Macy's parade. The most controversial it gets is when my father insists that Bullwinkle could kick Snoopy's ass. The only person to ever actually ask me if I'm gay is my sister, and she only brought it up because her then-boyfriend asked her if I was a queer. When I confirmed his suspicions, she was surprised, but not shocked. "It just never really occurred to me," she said in explanation. Then she told me about how the dog had just buried one of her shoes in the back yard, while I wondered if she'd really not noticed all the times I'd borrowed her lipstick when I was five.

I did sort of come out to my dad once. I did it by dedicating my book *The World Out There: Becoming Part of the Lesbian and Gay Community* to him. But I didn't tell him I did it. I just sent it to him and waited for the phone to ring. When it did, a few days later, he never mentioned the actual content of the book. All he said was that finally he had some payoff for funding my stay at college. Then he told me he'd just had to put his dog to sleep. I couldn't help but wonder if the tone of his voice suggested that the two events might not be entirely unrelated, but if it did he never said so. Besides, with the dog gone, we have no reason to call one another. Now he just sends postcards.

The fact is, my family just doesn't care one way or another. No one regrets that the family line will end with me. No one suggests that another grandchild would be nice. I think they're just happy that I'm not in prison, which they all suspected was a definite possible career path for me when I showed no interest in actually working for a living.

Because of this I have given up on the idea of creating a memorable life experience by coming out to anyone else in my family. To tell the truth, I'm a little jealous of my friends who have such stories. My friend Maxine, for example, came out while she was in the shower and her mother opened the door and asked, "Maxie, are you a lesbian?" My friend James still gloats that when we were in college together, the officials at our fundamentalist Christian school tried to deliver him from the demons they said caused his homosexuality by laying hands on him and praying, while no one even blinked when I put naked pictures of Kevin Costner on my dorm room walls or, for my final in public speaking, argued passionately against the biblical view of queerness as a sin. While James gained notoriety and the satisfaction of having scandalized the entire school, I got an A in public speaking and a deep-seated bitterness at not being infamous.

My mother and the whole Billy Graham thing was really my last shot at having a coming-out story that was even remotely interesting. I'm rapidly heading toward

30, and after that age no one cares anymore what you are. They just want to know why you aren't rich and famous yet. But our Billy Graham–Ryan White interaction was a bust.

Since then I've even attempted to manufacture a good outing story. Now I tell anyone who will listen, in the hopes that one of them will give me something to work with.

"I'll think about it," I told the telemarketer who called one night trying to get me to switch phone services. "But first I think there's something you should know—I'm gay."

"We don't discriminate," she said cheerfully. "You can still have the flat rate. Plus we donate a percentage of the profits to GLAAD."

"These boots fit really well," I assured the salesman at the mall last weekend. "But you do know that I'm gay, don't you?"

"That's fine," he said calmly. "We sell leather jackets too."

Not even the Jehovah's Witnesses who came by the house were thrown off, referring me to their recently created lesbian and gay affinity group. "They're having a potluck on Friday," said the nice lady as she handed me a copy of *The Watchtower* and her friend complimented me on my rose garden. Billy Graham should take note.

It used to be that coming out was a big deal. Parents became agitated. Friends reacted with surprise. People told complete strangers about the nice boy down the street who turned out to be "that way" or the girl they knew who caused her dear mother so much sorrow. There were entire books written telling us how to do it effectively and painlessly, and there were even books for the people we told, with activities designed to help them work through their feelings about it all. A good coming-out story was a badge of honor, a rite of passage for proud queers everywhere.

Now nobody cares. OK, maybe they care about Ellen or George Michael, but not about me. Not a single one of them. Not the mailman. Not the bus driver. Not even my dentist, and he sticks his hands in my mouth. I've come out to all of them this month, and no one has even blinked.

I know this is a good thing. After all, doesn't it mean that homosexuality is starting to lose some of the negative associations it once had? It's great that young queer people are declaring their sexuality in high school, and some even in middle or elementary school. I'm waiting for the first baby to be born clutching pride rings in its upheld fist. I'm happy for these people who have it easier than many their predecessors.

But I can't help but feel sorry for those of us who never got a chance to come out. What are we supposed to do? While some of you go around the room reminiscing about how grandma wrote you out of her will or how the bar mitzvah just wasn't the same after Billy Jacobson told the assembled guests what the two of you were doing behind the catering tent, those of us who are coming-out challenged sit in silence, hoping no one will notice. If you do call on us, we're forced to mumble something vague about how hard it was and hope no one will dig deeper. So the next time you have a pride picnic or holiday get-together and the talk turns to memories of self-revelation, remember those among us who might not have the most dramatic of stories to tell. We're still your brothers and sisters.

In the meantime, did I tell you what the dog did last night?

Part Five
Our Queer Lives

Generation Gap

I wish Larry Kramer would shut up.

Really, every time I open a gay newspaper or magazine, there's Larry complaining about something else. He's mad that, in his opinion, there's no real body of gay literature. He's mad that every single queer artist isn't devoting her or his entire life to talking about AIDS. He's mad that Yale University, his alma mater, turned down his offer of a multimillion-dollar bequest to establish a full-time gay studies professorship. He's even mad at Barbra Streisand—for not dropping everything and getting to work on the film version of his play *The Normal Heart.*

Most of all, Larry is mad at younger gay men. He's mad at them because, despite all of his screaming and ranting over the last 15 years, they're still not taking being gay seriously enough for his liking. Ever since his 1977 novel *Faggots,* which bitterly skewered gay male life and its obsession with beauty, sex, and youth, Kramer has been telling us that we don't have our priorities straight, that we should be spending less time being fabulous and more time fighting for gay causes and working toward the goal of gay equality and the recognition of gay accomplishments.

Well, duh.

Does he really believe that we don't know this? Apparently he does, because he hasn't stopped yelling at us yet. He did slow down a bit around 1980. But then, as though purposefully designed to prove Kramer's point, AIDS came along and gave him something new to be angry about. See, he said, I told you so. If you hadn't been out there dancing and drugging and boinking each other up the behinds in the baths, this would never have happened to us. Like a self-righteous parent, he stood before us with a disapproving look on his face, daring us to talk back and deny the truth he laid at our feet like the carcass of a freshly killed dear.

This started a whole new round of screaming and finger-pointing, one that has lasted for well over a decade now. It's even spawned a thriving new intellectual industry—the gay culture wars. On college campuses across the country and in the pages of thick and stupefying books, the pundits prattle on. Those who advocate freedom of sexual expression without limits as the cornerstone of gay politics label those calling for restraint puritanical and sexphobic. Those demanding a focus on monogamy and community action accuse the hedonists of rashness and irresponsibility. It's all very exciting, especially when they talk loudly.

And also very useless. What both sides have managed to completely ignore is that they're attempting to do what straight parents have done for centuries: trying to get the next generation to avoid making the same mistakes they themselves made. Only because we're all gay, we're pretending that we're the only group of people this has happened to. You know, kind of like what we've done with AIDS and homophobia and gay rights.

Larry Kramer thinks that by screaming at us and showing us all that a lot of people made mistakes that had consequences, that maybe we'll stop doing those things, or at least those of us who haven't done them yet will. And he isn't alone. There's a growing list of gay figures who have had grand epiphanies about the baseness of modern gay life and are fervently attempting to hold a mirror up to the gay community and show us our drunken, slutty selves in the hopes that we'll be so appalled at how we look that we'll hop right in the shower, throw on some decent clothes, and run out to help an elderly queen cross the street.

Unfortunately there's a tiny hitch to this plan, which is that people rarely learn from the mistakes of others. While in most respects I am probably Larry Kramer's perfect example of a writer who has failed to devote his life to documenting the crisis facing our community, I have done a few things he might approve of on a good day. For one, I wrote two books for young people about AIDS. Both books featured a number of interviews, and I talked to dozens of young people living with the effects of HIV. For the first book, which was written in 1991, the young people I spoke with said that they didn't have enough information about AIDS to know how to protect themselves. When I went to do a second book, in 1994, it was a different story. This time, the kids said that they knew all about HIV, but they just didn't think getting it could happen to them because they were too rich/white/educated/straight/cool/whatever.

I wasn't surprised. After all, how many times had my father warned me about driving too fast on the dirt roads by our house when I was 16 and freshly licensed? But it took skidding off the road, through a fence, and nearly into a river before I learned my lesson. And in college, even though I'd seen what happens when someone drinks vast quantities of alcohol, that didn't stop me from downing an entire bottle of gin and then bringing it all back up in a spectacular two-hour show that left me breathless and gagging.

In general, we all know what's good for us: eating right, exercising, driving cautiously, improving our minds, forming loving relationships, blah, blah, blah.

And we all know what's bad for us: smoking, excessive drinking, drugs, speeding, dysfunctional relationships, blah, blah, blah. Every one of those bad things can kill us, usually slowly and fairly quietly so that often we don't even notice. But some of us do them anyway, and some of us do at least two or three of them, probably on a daily basis. But having that pointed out to us isn't going to make us stop doing them, just like looking at all those pictures of diseased lungs and bloody car accidents in junior high didn't keep most of us from lighting up and driving too fast, at least once in a while. That more of us didn't die from it is pure dumb luck.

I agree with Kramer and those like him on some points. I do think a lot of gay men, especially young ones, think too much about being fabulous and too little about being well-rounded. I do think gay culture often emphasizes sex to the exclusion of other, more positive things. I do think that the promise of a cure for AIDS, or at least a prolonging of life with the virus, has made some of us grow careless. But I disagree with Kramer on how to change those things. Yelling at people doesn't help. Telling them what they should be doing with their lives—or with their art—doesn't help. Because they're going to keep on doing it anyway. They have to. That's what people do. We run around with scissors until we fall and hurt ourselves. Then most of us get right back up and do it again.

In a recent article Kramer raged that he hadn't worked so hard all of these years so that young gay men could go out and make the same mistakes that he and the men of his generation did. Well, guess what, Larry? They're going to do it anyway. Not because they don't believe you, but because they have to see it for themselves. Yes, they know it could kill them. Yes, they know it's a waste of time. So do all of those people who eat red meat, smoke cigarettes, drink too much, and snort piles of coke. Being self-destructive isn't the private property of queers. Neither is not listening to the words of people who have been through it all before. If it's any consolation, even if AIDS and drugs and all those other things were gone, someone would think of something else to get into trouble with. Just ask Eve about that apple.

Kramer has said his anger is what has kept him alive for so long. I'm sure he thinks of himself as a crusader, a voice of reason in a babbling crowd. But to me he seems more like the kid who insisted on telling everyone aboard the *Titanic* just how much water there was in the hold, even as the lifeboats were dropped into the sea. I can't help but wish he'd used the time a little more wisely. Instead of using his talents to create new work or to realize that life continues to go on even in the face of mass destruction, he's used every free breath to criticize, to complain, and to condemn. Perhaps it's left him a happy, fulfilled man, but I have my doubts. I mean, really, even Anne Frank managed to remember how good laughing felt.

Kramer has given me a lot of unasked-for advice over the years, so here's a little piece of advice for him and those like him: Take a lesson from parents (maybe not yours, but someone's) and lighten up a little. Stop wasting your time yelling at the kids and telling them what they're doing wrong. Try telling them what they're doing right. If they aren't doing anything right, try showing them what's worth caring about. But you're going to have to let them make mistakes on their own. No, it isn't pretty, and sometimes they're going to get hurt. That's what having kids means. But you aren't their savior, and you're missing out on the rest of your life while you worry about theirs. Suffering for the sins of the world might be noble if you're striving for sainthood, but ignoring the beauty around you is the biggest sin of all.

Most of all, stop banging your head against the wall over what you aren't changing. As my mother can tell you, all you're going to end up with is a headache and a dented wall. Larry, take those millions Yale doesn't want and throw yourself the biggest goddamn party you've ever had. I'll bring the records.

Send in the Clones

In 1979 Pat Benatar released her stunning debut album, *In The Heat of the Night*. This blockbuster featured a string of hits, including "Heartbreaker," "I Need a Lover," and "We Live for Love." The album is notable both because it launched Benatar's career and broke open the doors of rock to women and because it's a classic example of powerhouse songwriting.

But the record may be more important for another reason, the impact of which is just now being felt. See, tucked in between the smashes was an unnoticed song, a quirky little number called "My Clone Sleeps Alone." Stupidly forgettable, the lyrics were essentially a futuristic discourse on the erotic pleasures of the test-tube variety. "No VD, no cancer, on TV's the answer," went the first verse. "No father, no mother, she's just like the other." Benatar, who cowrote the song, envisioned a world where happiness came in the form of genetically engineered perfect lovers free of any worries. To sum up: "No sorrow, no heartache, just clone harmony. So obviously, it's heaven."

At the time we listened (this was before CDs allowed you to skip irritating tracks) and chuckled at the absurdity of it all. The notion of making love to a clone was all very exciting and *Blade Runner,* but surely it was reserved solely for science fiction movies. Besides, if our clones were as cranky as Daryl Hannah and Rutger

Hauer were to Harrison Ford, we weren't quite sure we wanted anything to so with them.

But now we have this sheep thing happening. And the monkey thing. It seems as though every day brings some new creature that's been genetically Xeroxed. Dolly the ewe now has several copies of herself scampering about, and there doesn't seem to be any stopping her or the folks who made her. You can't turn on the television without seeing yet another debate about the subject, with both sides arguing forcefully for their position. Bill Clinton is so upset by it that he's already trying to pass legislation to make sure we don't start doing it to people.

Guess what, Bill, it's too late. Queers have been cloning for years, and no one even noticed.

I know you've seen them—those scary couples who look disconcertingly like twins. Matching crew cuts. Duplicate smiles. Identical rainbow bracelets. They dance in pairs, looking only at one another as though staring lovingly into a mirror. They lounge beside one another at parties, a matched set for all to marvel at. They walk down the street hand in hand, making everyone wonder: Are they brothers?

Let's face it, some of us are a narcissistic bunch. We spend hours at the gym and tanning salon, Macy's and L.L. Bean, putting it all together and trying to look just so. When we've finally achieved the look we desire, whatever it is, we want to enjoy it to the fullest. So who better to partner with but ourselves? Since we can't find that exact duplicate, we go for the next best thing, someone who looks just like us. It's not perfect, but it's close.

I blame this whole gay clone obsession—along with many other horrors—on the '70s. Before then everyone pretty much looked alike, but in a generally bizarre hippie kind of way. Gay and straight people alike had long hair and tie-dyed clothing because we were all one big happily stoned family. Queers weren't particularly keen on being noticed, so we didn't see any reason to stand out. Besides, we were too busy trying to find places to pee at all the outdoor rock festivals.

But the '70s were different. Thanks to Stonewall we were starting to let people know that we were out there. We were thinking about the whole notion of being a community, and we needed a way to show our numbers. For the first time we felt like being our own unique selves right out in the open. And we had the Village People to show us the way.

Thus was the clone born into all his glory. Faded jeans, white T-shirt, mustache, aviator sunglasses, and work boots. Single earring optional, and leather jacket depending on the climate. He was a marvelous sight walking down the streets of New York and San Francisco. For festive occasions, he came equipped with some cunning metal-and-leather accessories and hankies of various shades, making dress-up fun. This early model, the Clone 1000, was extremely popular, especially with those of us who enjoyed sex in men's rooms and in the back seats of Gremlins. In fact, vintage models are still greatly in demand, and I sense a renewed interest in this style.

But the Clone 1000 was not without his problems. The sunglasses made eye contact difficult, and he had a tendency to overindulge in substances that made him difficult and uncooperative. While his leather outfits were fun to play with, the Crisco he favored for play tended to invade his sheets and leave stains on whatever it touched. Still, he was a marvelous dancer and was generally forgiven his occasional faults.

But he was not to last. Inevitably, tastes change, and with the dawning of the '80s the Clone 1000 fell on hard times. While many of the older models were still to be found, they were increasingly outnumbered by a newer line. The Clone 2000 was younger, sharper, and more aggressive. He had a well-paying job, wore designer clothes, and was powered by a new fuel—cocaine. Dancing the nights away to the fresh sounds of synthesized music, he thumbed his nose at the Clone 1000.

While the Clone 2000 may have been technologically more advanced, he lacked the spirit of the Clone 1000. Icy and aloof, he was unable to give off the same aura of excitement and danger. His music was edgy but sterile, and the sex he favored was less about sweat and heat than it was about cash and designer sheets. In trying to be the clone of the future, he had thrown out a little too much of the past.

As a result, his reign was short, and in the latter half of the '80s he found himself replaced by the sleeker Clone 2050. This model combined many features from both of the earlier editions, resulting in a clone that embraced his history while updating it for a new, tougher era. Back came the leather jackets and the white T-shirts. Back came the short hair. The fuel of choice was the hopefully named ecstasy.

The Clone 2050 quickly took over in gay communities around the country. Everywhere you looked you would see them, walking in groups completely indistinguishable from one another. While this was, for some of us, very disconcerting, it did have its advantages. For example, if one could adopt the look of the Clone 2050, one would find oneself with a limitless supply of friends and lovers. Since they were all named Todd, you only had to remember one name, and yelling it loudly at gatherings would guarantee any number of successful responses. And since they were all waiters, befriending one would ensure that you almost never had to pay for dinner.

Again, though, there were complications with this clone. Achieving the high-maintenance look of the Clone 2050 required hours at the gym and in tanning beds. For those of us who had jobs outside the food service industry and thus did not enjoy the benefits of flexible hours, this meant cutting back on almost all other activities. While we were generally able to get ourselves to look like the Clone 2050s, we found it difficult to actually keep up with them for any extended period. While shortly after midnight we faded into the backseats of taxicabs and went home for some much-needed sleep, they were just beginning to enjoy the thrill of the Junior Vasquez extended dance remix of Madonna's latest headache-inducing single. As a result, most of us never actually slept with a Clone 2050, finding ourselves, well, just too tired.

The '90s were a better time in the clone department. Perhaps due to the influence of Generation X, we began to diversify. While previous clones had come in only one basic model, the Clone 3000 came in a variety of shapes and sizes. Like Barbie and her friends, the Clone 3000 appeared on the streets dressed in leather *and* in suits. He masqueraded as a cowboy, a civil rights lawyer, and even as a frat boy. Sometimes he even appeared with children at his side, trading the Daddy version of the Clone 1000 for the more 1990s Dad variant.

But whatever guise he took, the Clone 3000 shared one basic trait with earlier models—he still only dated his own kind. He might come in a rainbow of forms, but when it came time to mate, he looked for someone just like himself. The cowboy clone found other range riders to bunk with, and the civil rights lawyer clone sought out another man who wore the same size 42 regular suit. Even the Dad clone scoured the country for another Dad, forming families whose holiday cards featured portraits of smiling children framed on either side by identically balding Clone 3000 fathers. For those of us who couldn't find our missing halves, it was a lonely time indeed.

As we stand poised to enter the 21st century, the clone problem may be solved once and for all. Whereas once the possibility of finding a partner was limited by the number of look-alikes roaming the streets of one's particular city, now there will be no shortages. Every gay man who desires a partner will have one at the ready. Why, we could even have two or three made up, just in case something happens to one of them. All we have to do is scrape a few cells from our tongue and let science do the rest. Then just think about the possibilities. No more arguing about Kenneth Branagh versus Jean-Claude Van Damme flicks. No squabbling over Thai or pizza, ballet or baseball. No more agonizing about just what it is he sees in us. Because he *is* us. As Pat predicted, it will be heaven.

Or will it. Sure, making love to yourself might be a thrill. But what if you find out that you just aren't that good in bed? And imagine if you realize after a few weeks of bliss that you really get on your nerves. Could you accept the fact that don't like yourself all that much? Worst of all, if the relationship doesn't work out, for once you really will have no one to blame but yourself. Do you really want that responsibility?

But wait. Maybe this cloning thing could be good for something else. Maybe we could use it to answer that old nature versus nurture question. We could take a queer (let's call him Todd), clone him, say, four or five times, and raise each of the kids in a different environment. Todd 1 would be raised by an overbearing mother and a father who doesn't play catch with him. Todd 2 would be raised by a nurturing mother and father (are there any?). Todd 3 would be raised by a single mom. Todd 4 would be raised by gay dads. Todd 5 would be raised by Catholic priests.

All the Todds would be carefully but unknowingly watched by a team of scientists, who would monitor

everything from their reading habits and musical preferences to their interest in particular toys and the degree of
their decorating abilities. None of the Todds would
know about the others. On reaching maturity and the expression of sexual behavior, the results of the experiment
would be examined to once and for all determine just
what or who makes a kid a homo. My money is on the
priests.

So go on—send in the clones. On second thought,
don't bother. They're already here.

The Waiting Game

So Brad Pitt and Gwyneth Paltrow, Hollywood's Golden Couple, have split up. Surprise, surprise. The gossip columnists are all in a state of shock. Fans are numb with the sudden demise of what appeared to be a sure thing. Not me. I knew it would happen.

Why? Because I know that if you wait long enough, anyone you want will become available. It's just a matter of having a little patience.

Do I sound jaded? No, just realistic. When I was younger and first testing out the waters of gay dating, I actually believed that if a man I was interested in had a lover, it meant he could never be mine. I didn't even give it a second thought. I just moved on.

But I quickly learned that true love is a fragile thing indeed. What seems like an indestructible union frequently has tiny fault lines running below the surface of the beautiful facade, just waiting for something to come along and crack it all into tiny pieces. Now I no longer assume that matching rings means don't touch or that a shared bed automatically implies domestic bliss.

The turning point came when a man I was intensely fascinated with told me there could never be anything between us because he was deeply in love with his partner of three years. As usual I believed him and forgot about the whole thing. At least until the night a few months later when he showed up at my door and within minutes the two of us were in the bedroom with our clothes a jumbled mess on the floor.

"But what about Kevin?" I said as he pounced on me.

"Oh, we broke up last week," he said cheerfully, and as his tongue entered my mouth, I began to rethink my original position on eternal devotion.

I might be more doubtful about my theory if that was an isolated incident. But it's a pattern I've seen repeated over and over, not just in my life, but in the lives of the people around me as well. Time and again I've heard friends—both male and female—wax longingly about the charms of this or that married object of desire. Then weeks, days, or even hours later, I see them walking hand in hand with the same formerly unavailable person. I am never surprised.

What is a bit frightening is the casualness with which breakups are expected now. Where even a few years ago the news that a potential flame was already attached would be cause for at least several hours of petulant sighing, now the most common response is, "Oh, well, I'll have to wait a couple of months then." The statement is made with no "maybes" attached to it. It is simply a fact. And 9½ times out of ten, it's true. The other one-half of a time, the relationship may remain intact, but occasional clandestine meetings can almost always be arranged.

To test this theory my friend Alice and I conducted an experiment. We made lists of five people we would happily date or at least sleep with if they weren't already in relationships. To keep things thoroughly scientific, we included in our groups people who had been in relationships for varying lengths of time.

My list looked like this:

1. Jake, 34, in a relationship for two years.
2. Ben, 26, in a relationship for six months.

3. Jeff, 30, in a relationship for five years.
4. Scott, 36, in a relationship for ten years.
5. Chuck, 32, in a relationship for a week.

Alice's list looked like this:

1. Milly, 28, in a relationship for two months.
2. Alicia, 40, in a relationship for 12 years.
3. Sophia, 34, in a relationship for a year.
4. Janet, 30, in a relationship for four years.
5. Chuck, 32, in a relationship for a week.

OK, so we both had Chuck on our lists. It isn't my fault that Alice is bisexual. Anyway, it made the game more fun. The object was to see how long it took before our various paramours became available. We defined available as either totally broken up and therefore thrown back into the dating pool or gotten into bed regardless of current marital status. The point was to see how long the vows of monogamy (all of our couples claimed fidelity) could be kept. Our only rule was that Alice and I couldn't do anything to directly break up the couple.

After the first month I had slept with two of the people on my list, while Alice had bagged one. My first was Ben, a man I had met one day as he jogged around the park and I let Roger chase the ducks in the pond. Ben had been shirtless, and the sweat made the hair on his belly swirl around like the starry night sky in a Van Gogh painting. I had been speechless, and when he stopped to ask Roger's name, I had to check the dog's tag before I could remember it. But before I could even think to ask him out, he'd told me that he and his lover were thinking of getting a dog and would love a Lab.

Now, perhaps his age made Ben more vulnerable to the wandering bug, but no one forced him into the trees behind the boathouse that afternoon at the park a week after Alice and I began our experiment. I merely suggested that it was extremely hot out and that Ben looked like he could use some cooling off. The rest of it was his idea. As for Jeff, the second to fall to the marriage test, he broke up with his lover, Bill, on their fifth anniversary, when Bill presented him with a bread maker instead of the Alaskan cruise Jeff was hoping for. I can't help it if he came over to tell me about it and I asked if a nice massage would make him feel better.

Alice's first turned out to be Janet, a coworker at the food co-op in town. Alice had had the hots for Janet ever since she saw her hoist a 100-pound bag of unprocessed oats onto one shoulder and carry it to the bulk foods aisle all by herself. But she didn't think she could ever compete with Janet's lover, a beautiful dancer who made her own soy cheese and developed a home-based business employing single lesbian mothers.

So imagine Alice's surprise when one day after she and Janet stayed late to unpack cartons of unbleached cotton sanitary pads, Janet offered her a sip of her iced herb tea. The next thing Alice knew she was on her back on a bag of basmati rice with Janet moaning "Mommy needs it bad" in her ear. Only later did Alice discover that Janet and her girlfriend had split up after a disagreement over Central American politics.

Encouraged by our early results, we expected the rest of the names on our list to succumb within weeks. But it would be some time before our next conquests. Alice managed to get two of hers at once when she discovered that Alicia had left her lover of a dozen years to take up with Milly and that the two of them were busily exploring the vast expanse of their desires by hosting lesbian sex parties in the basement of Alicia's recently remodeled Victorian house. Even as Alice repositioned herself on the cushions so as to get equal access to both of her newfound partners, she was crossing their names off her list and looking ahead.

I was not so lucky. It took another six months before I was able to get into bed with Jake and score my third victory. Jake and his lover, also named Mike, had been inseparable since meeting during a hike sponsored by the gay outdoor club they both belonged to. They even had matching red Jeeps. But then one afternoon Jake came home early to discover a blue Jeep in the driveway and someone named Bart in his and Mike's bed. With Mike. And they were wearing the matching baseball hats Jake had bought for himself and Mike on their first date. It was all too much for Jake to take, and he packed his stuff into his red Jeep and moved out that night, leaving Bart, the blue Jeep, and the now-soiled baseball cap with Mike.

Alice neared the end of her list when she went to Sophia's shop for a tarot reading one day and the cards said a younger woman would soon be entering her life. A couple of weeks later, after Sophia split up with her girlfriend, who, she discovered, was selling crystals from the store to support her drug habit, the identity of that young girl was revealed. And I was able to put a check mark next to Scott's name one wintry evening when he stopped by to return a book he'd borrowed and informed me that his lover, Paul, had accused him of having an affair with me, and while that was a totally ridiculous thing to say, maybe we should go ahead and do it since clearly Scott was going to have to pay for it anyway.

So there we were, nearing the one-year mark on our little experiment, and we'd crossed off all but one name on our lists. I won't go into too much detail about what happened with Chuck, but let's just say that before summer came again both Alice and I completed our halves of the deal within hours of one another. We celebrated by going out to dinner at our favorite restaurant, where we toasted our success and made plans for our follow-up experiment. After all, it's important to back up your initial test results.

While some unkind people might imply that the experiment merely proves that sluts are sluts and relationships are quite another thing altogether, I beg to differ. I prefer to wonder what Alice's and my success rate and the failure rate of the couples involved in our clinical trial say about us as a community. I suppose it depends on which side you're on. The religious right would, I have no doubt whatsoever, use it as proof that there's no such thing as stable gay relationships. Our seeming inability to remain forever faithful or even partnered long enough for the warranty on the blender to expire, would, to them, be evidence enough to support the theory that same-sex unions are simply not to be.

On the opposite extreme, supporters of gay marriage would likely argue that providing the same benefits to same-sex couples that are already available to opposite-sex couples would provide a stable framework on which to build the solid relationships we need. An interesting theory, and as a writer, I for one would welcome the possibility of sharing in a partner's health insurance. But as for such an arrangement fostering fidelity, I have my doubts. After all, heteros have had those benefits for hundreds of years, and as far as I can see, the only real outcome has been increased profits for lower-end motel proprietors, a never-ending supply of guests for "I Have a Secret to Tell You" *Ricki Lake* episodes, and anxiety-riddled children who have to split their holidays between Aspen and South Beach. As queers, we might not have all the benefits, but the fallout from our divorces is a lot less costly. Antique quilt racks can always be replaced, and shih tzus don't care who they live with as long as they're fed. Besides, we have the ex–Jackson-Parises to show us the way.

And it isn't just queers, anyway. As I mentioned earlier, look at Gwyneth and Brad. They were Hollywood's perfect couple. Sure, they can be forgiven for calling it quits. I mean, they weren't even married yet. But they're not the sole examples. My parents waited for more than 30 years before going their separate ways. And for years I've lusted after Bruce Willis. My friends all told me I didn't have a chance. "He loves Demi!" they cried. "They have three kids and a dog and a six-picture production deal with Sony!" Now just this morning I heard a rumor that he and Demi might be separating.

It looks like my new list is about to get shorter.

A Real Doll

By now everyone knows about Billy, the World's First Out and Proud Doll. Yes, as if rainbow flags, gay credit cards, and Ellen weren't enough, we now have our own doll. Or at least the first one to be really successful. Back in the '70s we had Gay Bob, but he never really caught on. I always blamed his bad perm and poor wardrobe, although he still maintains it was lack of support from the other dolls that did him in.

Billy, on the other hand, has a fantastic wardrobe. Probably because he was created by British fashion designer John McKitterick, who originally used Billy to model versions of his own clothes. McKitterick's friends thought the doll was so fabulous that they encouraged McKitterick to mass produce them. Now he has, and Billy has emigrated from the U.K. to the colonies, where he's disappearing (at around $49.95 a pop) almost as quickly as stores can stock him.

Standing 12 inches high, Billy is slightly larger than G.I. Joe, which means that if they ever move in together they'll have a hard time sharing clothes. And what clothes Billy has. He's available in five different versions: San Francisco Billy (with freedom rings and flannel shirt), Wall Street Billy (pinstripe suit), Sailor Billy (jaunty hat and white button-fly trousers), Master Billy (leather), and Cowboy Billy (the usual getup). If you buy all five, you can form your own Billy version of the Village People.

I don't know about the rest of you, but as a kid I was fascinated by action figures (that's what boys call dolls). They were like playing with really little people. I remember that my G.I. Joe had real peach-fuzz hair and beard, which I loved to rub against my cheek until the day my best friend's baby brother sucked on Joe's head, creating the action figure version of male pattern baldness. Undaunted, I stuck a hat on Joe's head, and off he went on another adventure.

See, that was the whole point of G.I. Joe. He had adventures, and we got to go along. To this end, he came with a never-ending series of outfits and accompanying paraphernalia, including parachuting ensembles, jungle action gear, a wet suit, and even swim trunks. I spent hours hanging him from trees (parachuting accident), burying him in the mud (quicksand), and hurling him through the air (airplane ejection seat). It was all too thrilling.

I wonder if Billy will have such an exciting life. Maybe, like Barbie, he'll eventually come with a series of friends, like Robert and Bruce, the slightly bitchy long-term couple he meets on Sundays for brunch. Or perhaps Todd, the overly tanned best buddy with whom Billy spends Saturday evenings at the Club Boy module, which will come equipped with flashing lights, loud techno music, and realistic smoke smell. And for those who don't appreciate Billy's pointedly stereotypical look, there could be Just Like Everyone Else Billy. He looks exactly like Ken, but he comes with his own copy of *A Place at the Table*.

When Billy first came out, I worried most about his love life. Unlike G.I. Joe and Ken, Billy is realistically (and hugely) endowed, which creates all kinds of interesting prospects. Envision, for example, Master Billy at the Dungeon. This cunning set could feature fully functional slings, paddles and whips made to scale, and even a secret back room. Or for the more vanilla Billy, there would be the Fire Island play set, sporting an overpriced weekend share, condoms in assorted colors, and a stunning ensemble (complete with heels and Carmen Miranda hat) to be worn at Sunday Afternoon Drag Tea Dance. But unless Billy was willing to have sex with his twin, or with the sexless Joe and Ken dolls, he was out of luck.

But recently Billy was given a lover. His name is Carlos, the World's First Out and Proud Boyfriend, and he's just as hunky as Billy is. Even hunkier, actually. Unlike Billy, who has a slightly mongoloid appearance, Carlos is a walking Tom of Finland character. He has hair on his chest and a charming Vandyke beard that makes him irresistible. In fact, most stores are having a hard time keeping him in stock, as it seems all across the country gay men are falling madly in love with him.

I'm very excited about this Billy-Carlos relationship, because it presents a lot of new options. Now that they've hooked up, they can do all of those things that real gay couples do. They can go on a lovely RSVP cruise to the Bahamas, and it will be easy to fill up the boat with other dolls because you can just use lots of Kens. Never mind that they all look alike. This simply creates a remarkably authentic simulation of a real RSVP trip. You can also send Billy and Carlos to an AIDS walkathon or, by grouping lots of Billys and Carloses together, enable them to form a gay men's chorus to entertain the other dolls on holidays and during gay pride. My personal favorite afternoon activity would be to send Billy and Carlos to a sold-out Spice Girls dolls concert. But that's just me.

The creator of the Barbie doll said in a recent interview that the entire purpose of the doll was to give little girls a way to act out what they wanted their lives to become. By turning their inner fears and fantasies into games that Barbie could play, they would be able to cope with their feelings about becoming adults.

I think Billy and Carlos could do the same thing for gay men that Barbie has done for generations of young girls. Imagine if we were able to take all of the stressful situations of our queer lives and turn them into scenarios that Carlos and Billy could act out for us. How much easier would it be to have Billy confront Carlos over the crumpled-up phone number discovered in Carlos's jeans pocket by Billy when he went to do the wash than it would be to do the same with our real-life boyfriends? Why not let Billy and Carlos fight with G. I. Joe and Ken about which house to rent for the trip to Russian River? And when we encounter breakups in our own lives, wouldn't they be easier to cope with if we had the support of Carlos, the World's First Out and Proud Ex-Boyfriend? By reducing these kinds of confrontations to the level of play, we could make solving our day-to-day problems easier, maybe even fun.

The possibilities are many. But the big question is: Will Billy and Carlos get into the hands of those who need them most, namely prepubescent queens? A few years ago, when I was living in New York, some enterprising souls bought up a bunch of talking Barbies and talking G.I. Joes. You remember the talking Barbie, she said outrageous things like, "Math class is tough." It was a national scandal.

Well, these folks solved the problem by switching Barbie's microchip with G.I. Joe's, so that now Joe had a hard time with math and what to wear on his date with Ken, and Barbie got to say things like, "Let's get Cobra Commando! Go Joe!" in a voice just slightly less butch than Bea Arthur's. They then put all the dolls back into their respective boxes and returned them to the stores just in time for the holidays. That Christmas, a lot of unsuspecting kiddies pulled out their dream presents and had a little lesson in gender reversal.

Had I received one of those Joes as a child, my life might have been a bit easier. And who knows what might have happened if Billy and Carlos had been around. I loved my G.I. Joe, but he wasn't very helpful when it came to figuring out why it was that I wanted to play with my friend Stephanie's Easy-Bake Oven more than I wanted to play with my Lincoln Logs. While Joe would sit in mute disapproval of my homemaking skills, Billy and Carlos would gladly have given me their secret recipe for making the most amazing pineapple upside-down cake. And where Joe merely tolerated it when I slowly removed his Army uniform to get a glimpse of what was underneath, Carlos and Billy would have had no qualms about letting me get a look at their goods.

They would have been the gay friends I never had. Even better, they would have been the gay older brothers I never had, dispensing their advice when needed and giving me a helping hand when I was unsure of myself. "You're supposed to roll the sleeves of your T-shirt up," they would whisper helpfully when I was in doubt on the first day of school. On those nights when I felt like being alone with Ken, I bet Carlos and Billy would gladly have accompanied Barbie to the mall for some shoe shopping to get her out of the way. While I might have been disappointed to sometimes find one or the other of them giving G.I. Joe a blow job in Barbie's whirlpool while the other was off at the gym, I would have always looked the other way.

I can only imagine, then, what it might do for a young queen receiving a Billy or a Carlos doll on his birthday or Christmas. Surely a child who benefited from such playthings would grow up healthy and happy, able to skip those unpleasant years many of us spent trying to come to grips with our queerness. I might even get a chance to find out. My nephew shows all the signs of becoming a full-fledged queer. He sings along to Barbra Streisand albums. He redecorated his room using copies of *Martha Stewart Living*. Last year he asked for the cast recording of *Joseph and the Amazing Technicolor Dreamcoat* for his birthday. This year, he doesn't have to ask. I already know what to get him. I just have to decide whether he'd prefer Master Billy or San Francisco Carlos.

In & Out Rage

I am, in general, not a big fan of going to the movies. Being locked for 90 minutes or more in a small, sticky room with people I do not know and who insist on eating things that crackle does not make me happy. I much prefer waiting for things to come out on video. Even though I understand that things are not always as thrilling on the small screen as they are on a big one, and while my cinema-enthralled friends insist that bits of the movie are lost when it is formatted to fit my television, I think these are small concessions to make for the joy of being able not only to watch a movie at a reasonable volume but also to have the freedom to pee whenever I want to without missing anything.

Despite my misgivings, however, some months ago I was coerced into attending a screening of the Kevin Kline film *In & Out*. Someone of my acquaintance had won or been given tickets, and I was dragged along. Now, when I do go to the movies I tend to like things where buildings explode and hunky men run around shirtless. My attention span is very short, and anything that requires a lot of thought leaves me drained. While comedies are seldom overly taxing, I didn't know what to expect from this one, and I wasn't exactly looking forward to it.

Much to my surprise, I thoroughly enjoyed it. Sure, there were some holes in the plot, but who cared? Joan

Cusack was a scream as the bewildered bride who can't see the reality beyond her fiancée's love of Barbra Streisand. Debbie Reynolds had me howling with her portrayal of every mother who just wants to see her child married. And it was almost too much seeing Kline and Tom Selleck smooch. Tom was one of my first homo fantasies, and when I was growing up I kept hidden inside my Bible a drawing some artist had done of him nude. Kevin isn't half bad either, and as far as I was concerned, a good time was had by all.

Later in the week I went online to check my E-mail. Because I had a novel due the next day and it was nowhere near completion, this resulted in an hour or so spent looking at useless information on the Internet. Somewhere in my wanderings I stumbled on a folder devoted exclusively to people's thoughts on *In & Out*. Curious as to why such a thing would exist for such a lightweight movie, I spent some time reading through the postings.

To my surprise, nearly all were filled with anger and condemnation of the movie. The posters didn't like the "stereotypical" portrayal of gay men. They didn't like the fact that Tom Selleck's character wasn't entirely sympathetic. They didn't even like the fact that the Village People were on the soundtrack.

There was a lot of finger-pointing and blaming going on. People were mad at nongay Kevin Kline for doing the role. They were mad at gay writer Paul Rudnick for "selling out the community." They were mad at the gay people who laughed along at the film and at the straight people who laughed with them. Or, more precisely, who laughed *at* them. Because that was the problem everyone seemed to be having—we were being made fun of. "Why," wrote one fellow who pretty much summed up the tone of the messages, "can't Hollywood create a movie that depicts what the essence of being gay is instead of making us all look silly?"

I'll tell you why—because the essence of being gay *is* being silly, or at least understanding being silly. I don't care if you don't like hearing it. It's true. There's no deep cosmic secret about being gay. There's no arcane experience embedded deep within the heart of our gay souls just waiting to be revealed to the rest of the world. What being gay means is that we have a way of looking at life that is different from the way other people who do not go through life as gay people look at life. And for many of us, that means recognizing that the most positive way to deal with everything the world throws at you is to laugh at it. Have you learned nothing from Harvey Fierstein?

Unfortunately there seem to be a lot of queers who want our differences to go away, who want us all to be just like everybody else because then we'll be taken seriously. Sorry. I for one am really tired of gay people who use the word "stereotypical" when what they really mean is "what we're afraid of looking like." The word is almost always used to describe a gay character who is less than superbutch, who does drag, or who knows all the words to "Over the Rainbow." If the "stereotypical" character is a lesbian, she has short hair, plays softball, rides a motorcycle, and has at least three cats, two of whom are named Gertrude and Alice. The third is probably named after her ex-lover.

I hate to break it to you, folks, but there are a lot of "stereotypical" gay people running around. Even those of you who think you aren't like that probably have more of the Barbra queen in you than you think. And you know what—that's a great thing. These little in jokes, these common reference points, are things that bind us together as a group. Why do you think it's oh-so-easy to play Spot the Queer or Pin the Tail on the Dyke when you stroll through the mall or dine out at your local Denny's? Why do you think we can look at the 12-year-old boy who (as my nephew does) sews his own clothes and sings a flawless "Evergreen" and nod knowingly at one another. Like it or not, most of us in the great rainbow scout troop are just, well, somehow different from the other kids.

But still some of us persist in thinking that it's only other people who look gay or act gay or, well, *are* gay. I have a friend who for a time lived on San Francisco's quintessentially gay Castro Street. He was so ashamed of his address that he took a post office box so that no one would see his street address on his checks or on his mail and "think he was a faggot." I hate to break it to him, but despite the fact that he tries his best to distance himself from his swishy brothers, he doesn't exactly blend. But he still thinks no one knows about him. And from the uproar we hear every time Hollywood gives us yet another "stereotypical" gay character, he isn't alone.

There was, for a long time, a movement to change the image of the queer community. This was particularly noticeable in books written for young people about lesbians and gay men. Having written several books about gay issues for this audience myself, I've read most of what's available, and what has always disappointed me most was when I got to the part—and there was always a part—in which the author reassured the readers that stereotypes are not true. Great pains were taken to let young people know these were just images other people had of us and that we didn't have to be oppressed by them.

I agree with these authors on one point: Not all of us fit the common stereotypes. But a lot of us do. And while the kids who don't will surely feel better about themselves, those who are in fact big flaming queens and softball dykes will feel even worse when they think they've let the rest of us down somehow by being what everyone says they are.

I thought of this when I picked up the paper yesterday and read about an incident which occurred in Northampton, Mass., a few weeks ago in which a 15-year-old boy stabbed a 16-year-old classmate to death after enduring months of teasing. It seems the older boy decided the younger one must be a fag because he liked theater, wore flamboyant clothes, and once came to school sporting eyeliner. He taunted his victim one too many times, and ended up paying with his life.

The 15-year-old has not said whether he is in fact gay. Whether he is or not, I understand the rage that drove him to do what he did. When I was his age, I endured the same kind of relentless teasing from classmates because I wasn't good at sports, had a best friend who was a girl, and, worst of all, played the piano for the school chorus. I also, although none of my fellow students knew this, was obsessed with Bette Davis movies, and I sensed that had something to do with it as well. While now I often find myself being mistaken for a straight guy (it's the flannel shirts, I swear), back then I endured daily torment just walking from class to class.

I knew enough then to be angry at my classmates' ignorance and not at myself, but when you constantly want to pound some people into the ground, moral superiority doesn't really help. You need something more tangible. I still vividly recall driving my father's enormous pickup truck one day and seeing one of my chief persecutors walking along the road ahead of me. His back was to me, and he didn't know I was there. Without even thinking, I aimed the truck at him and hit the gas. For a long moment, as the truck sped straight for him, I felt absolutely nothing as I pictured his bloodied body sprawled on the gravel. It wasn't until I was right behind him that I finally swerved, narrowly missing him. As it was, he went sprawling into the ditch, but for days I was angry at myself for not being able to keep the wheel steady.

The point is, these kids had made me angry about what I was. So angry that I wanted to kill them. I sensed that who I was and what I was was OK. I knew they were the ones who were wrong. But I also knew that the teasing would stop if I were more like them. I wasn't willing to become different and let them win the battle, but I also wasn't so thrilled about the alternative. And there were no books telling me that there were other people like me out there and that I didn't have to change for anyone.

As I grew up, came out, and started becoming part of the gay world, I was surprised to find that many other men had experiences similar to mine. There were a lot of us who had been stereotypical fags back in our school days. But what I also found was that no one was really very proud of that. In fact, most of the men I met were very busy trying to become something completely different. Hours at the gym resulted in bodies that mirrored the masculine ideal. Great pains were taken to be invulnerable to suspicions of queerness from outsiders.

I understand this. Years of fighting makes you a little tired of having to do it constantly, and blending in is a relief. But what surprised me was the viciousness a lot of the men I met felt toward those of us who look and act like grown-up versions of the budding queers we were all those years ago. In particular, they were determined to find partners who had no such qualities. While they would call one another "she" and "girl" with ease, they claimed that they would have nothing but "straight-acting" men as lovers.

Straight-acting. It's a phrase I have come to love for its comic possibilities. You see it a lot in the gay world, generally in personal ads: "Straight-appearing/straight-acting seeks same. No fems need apply." It always makes me think for a minute as I imagine what exactly "straight-acting" means. Does it refer to a guy who likes to think he's always right just because he's a guy? Does it mean a man who will never ask for directions? Or is it a guy who, after you have sex, goes home to his wife and kids? I wish someone would explain it to me.

I wonder if these straight-acting guys ever really find one another? If they do, what are their relationships like? I can't help but picture them sitting around in their badly decorated split-level in the suburbs trying to decide whether to take their summer vacation at the Grand Canyon or Club Med. Undecided, they watch *60 Minutes* and talk about what a riot that Andy Rooney is before they call it a night.

I know, I'm being a little harsh on these straight-acting guys. I'm sure a lot of them are really nice fellows, and they can't help it if they don't know how to cook or dance. I can't dance, either. So maybe we have something in common after all. And I've had more than one man tell me he wanted to date me because I was "such a regular guy." Well, I may look like a regular guy and walk like a regular guy, but inside there's still a faggy little kid who sewed a quilt when he was ten and pounded out ABBA's "S.O.S." for the school's talent contest. And I myself am very fond of big, jocky types. But I want my man to be able to laugh at himself from time to time, to be able to enjoy the queeny side of life in all its glory. He doesn't have to do a great drag impression of Mae West, but I would like him to be able to appreciate one.

Yes, the Kevin Kline character in *In & Out* is a bit limp-wristed and prissy. Yes, he goes to the mat for La Barbra (at his bachelor party no less). Yes, he walks like a queen and talks like a queen and even kisses like a queen. That's why he's so wonderful. We can watch him and laugh at everything he does because we know that even if we aren't all exactly like him, there's a bit of him in all of us and a bit of each of us in him. He might not be in on the joke at first, but once he is, he realizes that he's fabulous the way he is and he doesn't care what the straight folks think (and they accept him anyway, because in addition to being gay he's a great guy). There are a whole bunch of uptight queers out there worried about what straight people will think of them if they act "too gay" who could learn something from him. And as for those of us who might just be "stereotypical" raging dykes and fags, I say rage on.

Once Upon a Time

Remember when being gay was fun?

When I was growing up in the '70s, I thought gay people were the coolest. My best friend, Stephanie, had a gay uncle named Fred. Fred had a mustache, wore jeans and T-shirts with work boots, and frequently drove us to Dairy Queen for hot fudge sundaes. On Friday nights Stephanie and I would beg Fred to take us roller-skating. As the Bee Gees and Alicia Bridges sang to us, we would circle the rink hand in hand, watching the gay men who swarmed around us and wishing we could be just like them. We weren't exactly sure what being gay was, but from the little we'd seen and heard on shows like *Three's Company,* we figured it must be thrilling beyond words.

As I got older I realized that I was, in fact, one of those men like Fred. While the prospect was a little bit scary, the idea pleased me to no end. In my room decorated with Shaun Cassidy posters and littered with copies of *Tiger Beat,* I listened to the Village People and imagined a life where men walked around in fabulous costumes and did exciting, if not entirely explicit, things with one another. I imagined myself in my T-shirts and work boots like Fred's and wondered how I'd look with a mustache.

Things changed slightly when I entered junior high and my family moved from an urban area to a small town in the New York countryside. It was the '80s. AIDS had just begun to appear in the news. The other students in my small-town school talked about "fags" and "lezzies" and how awful they were, even as they danced the night away to bands like Wham! and Culture Club. For a number of reasons, I was singled out as the school queer, and life was not particularly pleasant. Still, I knew being gay was something special, and I couldn't wait to get out of there and jump headlong into the queer world. I read Gordon Merrick novels and was both horrified and aroused by them. I watched *Making Love* and fantasized about kissing Harry Hamlin. I secretly sneaked downstairs to watch the documentaries on gay life shown by the local public television station each June, counting the years until I could be part of it myself.

After high school, I ended up in a college run by fundamentalist Christians. Homosexuality was not particularly encouraged there, and as a result what little gay life existed was kept deeply underground. The queer student body consisted primarily of the women's basketball and softball teams and a handful of repressed men who dated women but sneaked into one another's rooms at night for the action they really longed for.

Oddly, I loved the clandestine nature of gay life there. I liked being subversive (even if I was also invisible), and I liked knowing I was doing things (or at least thinking about things) the rest of the school would find appalling. I read books about gay history and was fascinated by the stories of bars with red lights over the doors to warn of police raids. The idea of belonging to a group of people who moved below the surface of society appealed to me greatly, despite the dangers associated with it.

When I graduated and was let out into the real world, I ended up in New York City, smack in the middle of Greenwich Village. Finally I was surrounded by the culture I'd been waiting my whole life for. Gay bars. Gay bookstores. Gay restaurants. All around me there were queer women and men living their queer lives. It was what I'd dreamed of as Stephanie and I whirled around beneath the glitter ball all those years ago. The first night I stood on a dance floor surrounded by sweaty men moving to the sounds of Janet Jackson, I remembered how Donna Summer had sounded when I was 12, and I felt as though I'd come home.

But there was something else going on in those days. As I read the magazines and newspapers I found all around me, I saw that more and more, the articles were about making demands. Queer people were demanding to be allowed to march in other people's parades. We were demanding that people listen to what we had to say. We were demanding that they pay attention to our writing and our art. We were demanding that people stop pointing at us and calling us names.

That's when I realized being queer was no longer about having our own little corner of the world. Now it was about making everyone be nice to us. It had become about fitting in.

We never used to care. We used to like being different. We thought it was really great to have our own music, our own books, our own style. It was our secret world. OK, so a lot of people didn't think very much of us. And a lot of times people were mean to us and did things like beat us up, take our children away, and fire us. They even blamed things like AIDS on us. So we fought back. We marched in the streets and carried signs into churches. We threw rocks. We stormed city halls across the nation. We took back the night, although the women of the Seven Sisters schools admittedly had the idea first.

And things did change. People started talking about us and what we were demanding. They stopped ignoring us. They stopped saying we were psychotic (officially). They stopped firing us (at least for being gay) and stopped taking our children away (some of the time).

They put us on magazine covers and invited us to speak at their conventions. They admitted (reluctantly) that we'd done some really cool things for them. They even gave some of us (the least offensive ones) things like Tony awards and Grammys.

But they haven't stopped hating us. Not really. They haven't stopped blaming us for things like AIDS. They haven't stopped beating us up or telling their children that if they turn out like us they'll make Jesus throw up. They might have cut down a little on calling us names to our faces, but when we aren't around, they still talk about what a pain in the ass we are and wish we would just shut up already. They've added us to their list of endangered species, but they still don't care if we survive. They pretend to invite us to their parties, but they hope we won't really come.

So was it worth it? In our bid for respectability, what have we given up? We used to have things like disco and John Waters. Now we have gay marriage and Andrew Sullivan. We used to have our own neighborhoods and our own style. Now even in the Village you can't always tell the queers from the straight wanna-bes who think it's fun to look like us. Straight culture has co-opted everything from our music to our kitsch. Even U2 thinks they're the Village People now, and last night I saw a commercial for Kraft macaroni and cheese featuring a contented housewife stirring her pot to the tune of Donna Summer's "Love to Love You Baby."

And what do we have to show for it? We've turned into a serious bunch of people who want to see our queerness as just another part of who we are, rather than as an essentially defining part. Instead of relishing what makes us unique, we want to see it as an accessory we can take off or put on depending upon how we want to appear to the outside world. If showing too much means getting disapproving glances, we tone it down a little.

We gather sympathetic straight celebrities around us and ask them to be our friends, so that everyone will see that we're really OK. We watch what we say and what we do, because we don't want to give anyone "the wrong impression" about what queers are really like. We want to be just like everyone else, because it makes us feel better.

I'm not saying that fighting for our rights isn't important. I'm not saying that there isn't important work to be done around homophobia and equality and making this a better place for queer youth. I'm not saying I'm not thankful for straight people who stick up for us once in a while.

But why do we have to achieve those things by pushing who we are into the background? Why do we have to be so thrilled when they give us a pat on the back after they've decided that maybe drag queens and inoffensive gay characters are OK because they play well in suburban multiplexes after all? Why do we have to pretend that the men in leather and the dykes on bikes in our pride parades are embarrassing, when secretly most of us wish we could be more like them, if only for a night? Why do we want everyone to like us so much?

Maybe I'm just cranky. But more and more, I feel like a kid at story hour. When I talk to gay men a decade older than myself, the conversation is peppered with phrases like "remember when" and "back in the old days." Those days are far from ancient history, and they were certainly far from perfect, but in many ways they might as well belong to the time of the Brothers Grimm. In this era of political correctness, avalanches of ribbons and causes, and debates over what's right for our community, the past has become something of a fairy tale. Increasingly, our gay pride festivities are more about lobbying and planning than they are about partying and letting loose, more dogged sign-waving than celebration.

At one of my first pride rallies in New York, I sat with

thousands of other queers as speaker after speaker got up and spoke about our rights and what we'd accomplished during the year in our campaign for respectability. The audience dutifully applauded after each one and shook their fists at appropriate times. So did I, all the time feeling guilty that what I was really feeling was boredom. I could have been at any rally for any group. I didn't feel special or different. I didn't care if Madonna and Tom Hanks liked me.

Then somewhere someone turned on some music. All of a sudden, the sounds of Gloria Gaynor's "I Will Survive" swept over the park. A great roar went up as a group of men, most of whom had probably heard the song when it was first played in a disco, stood up and started to dance. These were men who had been gay before AIDS, before we decided that getting married would make us respectable, before Madonna ever thought we were cool. They'd seen the wonderful highs and the awful lows. And they were dancing because it was fun and because it didn't have to mean anything.

At first people stared at them as they would a child who had just blurted out some horrible family secret in the middle of a dinner party. They'd broken the solemnity of the speeches and the earnestness of the moment. Then, slowly, throughout the park men and women jumped to their feet and began to join in, hands over their heads as they clapped and sang along. For a few minutes it was as though I was back in that roller rink. Only this time I was one of the men speeding by, happy to be different. It was a moment that could only happen when 7,000 queers stood up and reminded themselves that to be just like everyone else might be comforting, but it's a lot more fun to be different, even if it costs us something.

I hope we don't ever forget that.

alyson
books

A FRAGILE CIRCLE, *by Mark Senak.* The story of a man's love for his friends, his partner, and himself set against the backdrop of the AIDS epidemic.

B-BOY BLUES, *by James Earl Hardy.* A seriously sexy, fiercely funny black-on-black love story. A walk on the wild side turns into more than Mitchell Crawford ever expected. An Alyson best-seller you shouldn't miss.

DESMOND, *by Ulysses G. Dietz.* When gay vampire Desmond falls in love with a human man, his dark world will be forever changed.

THE GOOD LIFE, *by Gordon Merrick.* In 1943 a high-society murder case drew international attention for its irresistible combination of violent crime, scandalous sex, and enormous wealth. Gordon Merrick and Charles Hulse put their own fictional stamp on the story, and an entertaining romp through the lives of rich young gay men emerges. "Beautifully visual writing," says *The Washington Blade.*

JOCKS, *by Dan Woog.* An intriguing look at America's gay male jocks as the locker-room closet opens up. Is there life after coming out to your teammates? Is there life before coming out? This collection of more than 25 inspiring real-life stories digs deeply into two of America's twin obsessions: sports and sex.

LOVE BETWEEN MEN: ENHANCING INTIMACY AND KEEPING YOUR RELATIONSHIP ALIVE, *by Rik Isensee.* The only step-by-step self-help book specifically geared toward gay men in relationships.

MY FIRST TIME, *edited by Jack Hart.* Hart has compiled a fascinating collection of true stories by men across the country, describing their first same-sex encounters. *My First Time* is an intriguing look at just how gay men begin the process of exploring their sexuality.

These books and other Alyson titles are available at your local bookstore.
If you can't find a book listed above or would like more information,
please visit our home page on the World Wide Web at **www.alyson.com**.